Praise for

BROTHER & SISTER
ENTER THE FOREST

Finalist for the Lambda Literary Award for Gay Fiction

A *New York Times Book Review* Editors' Choice

"*Brother & Sister Enter the Forest* is an eerie, psychologically devastating novel by any measure, but it's Mirabella's careful, emotionally honest rendering of the ever-shifting relationship between older brother, Justin, and younger sister, Willa, that marks this book as a revelation."
—Christopher Bollen, *The New York Times Book Review*

"Part fantastical horror, part road trip narrative, *Brother & Sister Enter the Forest* is an uncanny portrait of the lengths we go to protect the people we love."
—Isle McElroy, *Vulture*

"Told with an incredibly steady hand, this novel dissects a tense sibling relationship. Carefully detangling life-shattering events from the pair's past, the book manages to look straight at its characters and show the shadows behind them. Like the careful dioramas that the sister makes in her spare time, this book is an exquisite creation, made carefully and precisely." —*Bustle*

"Spellbinding . . . Between Mirabella's expertise on the sentence level and the love he infuses into the story—a

T0190972

love that explores the liminal space between tragedy and triumph—the reader is quick to trust that this journey is a necessary one. *Brother & Sister Enter the Forest* is haunting and gorgeous, pensively exploring memory, family, and love's limits."   —Rachel León, *BOMB*

"Mirabella's debut novel—about a pair of once-close siblings and how the bruises of their youth swell into adulthood—is both bracing and a balm, his softly disarming sentences like cotton puffs that absorb the pain of deep cuts."
                    —Michelle Hart, *Electric Literature*

"Stunning . . . Mirabella's sentences ache in their simplicity . . . He shows readers the trauma of a mother who is quiet, even patient, in her homophobia. Of classroom bullies who are still around today. Of building a chosen family that disappoints. Of remembering—and not."
                    —Marissa Higgins, *The Rumpus*

"A strange, beautiful, and memorable book."
                    —Adam Vitcavage, *Debutiful*

"A meticulously woven narrative . . . This is a fairy tale of adulthood much like Hanya Yanagihara's more expansive but similarly austere *A Little Life*, both of which explore how childhood trauma can come to define a person for the rest of their days—as well as how it often bleeds into our relationships with others, warping them in its image . . . The quiet dazzlement on display here is in how he inverts the old saying, words speaking so much more loudly than action ever could." —Richard Scott Larson, *Slant*

"Literary star-on-the-rise Richard Mirabella delivers a powerful reckoning with past trauma, and the connections we forge amidst it all." —Greg Mania, *StyleCaster*

"Riveting, relentless. A novel of calm and chilling reserve and accomplishment." —Joy Williams, author of *Harrow*

"There are so many things to love about Richard Mirabella's outstanding *Brother & Sister Enter the Forest*, but what I love best is its meticulous attention to atmosphere, by which I mean the music of the book, the soul of it, expressed in its incisive descriptions, its cadence, its dark and tender heart. It's what revives me every time I pick it up, and it will keep me coming back again and again."
—Paul Lisicky, author of *Later: My Life at the Edge of the World*

"This is a gorgeous novel—full of mystery, dread and a deep, melancholy understanding of what it means to love someone who is mentally ill. I was completely captivated."
—Dan Chaon, author of *Sleepwalk*

"Richard Mirabella's debut novel, *Brother & Sister Enter the Forest*, doesn't so much seek understanding as it does carve indelible and brave circles into the depths of desire, violence, loss, and belonging that keep us alive, connected, heartbroken and in love, despite logic or consequence. This novel makes the world bigger."

—Madeline ffitch, author of *Stay and Fight*

"Befitting its fairy-tale title, *Brother & Sister Enter the Forest* sits in a mist of unease, haunted by the restless ghosts of childhood violence and abuse. But what lingers most in Richard Mirabella's masterful novel are the brilliant moments of tenderness between siblings, between lovers, between friends, between parents and children—all of them grasping for one another's hands in the face of so much pain, all of them fighting to meet life's messiness with compassion and love. This is brave, beautiful storytelling."

—Zak Salih, author of *Let's Get Back to the Party*

"A unique, evocative novel that doesn't shy away from awkwardness and pain. Mirabella's debut delves into the stubborn, haunted connections between his characters and those they've known and loved. A wry, original, new voice in fiction!"   —Rachel B. Glaser, author of *Paulina & Fran*

Brother & Sister
Enter the Forest

A Novel

..

RICHARD MIRABELLA

..

Catapult
New York

First Catapult edition: 2023
First paperback edition: 2024

Hardcover ISBN: 978-1-64622-117-2
Paperback ISBN: 978-1-64622-217-9

Library of Congress Control Number: 2022944542

Cover design by Sara Wood
Cover images: deer © Eva Carollo Photography / Getty Images;
trees © Gunther Kleinert / EyeEm
Book design by Wah-Ming Chang

Catapult
New York, NY
books.catapult.co

Printed in the United States of America

1 3 5 7 9 10 8 6 4 2

For my parents

BROTHER & SISTER
ENTER THE FOREST

Years ago, Willa's brother Justin lived in a house with four other men, and Willa went to visit him. Justin and a pair of dogs answered the door. The dogs rubbed against Willa's legs and Justin hurried to pull them away. They stood inside the door for a moment. It surprised her that everything looked so clean and organized. The large silver refrigerator in the kitchen gleamed and there wasn't a single dish or glass in the sink. The sun lit up every room Justin brought her to; no lamps were turned on.

The four other men were there. One of them, with an ugly dent in his forehead, shook her hand and welcomed her to the house. It amazed her what people could survive. Justin introduced him, but his name slipped away. She didn't need it. She didn't like to think of Justin as an addict, but he said he was an addict. To live in this house, you had to have lost control. She didn't know all the details, but he had been arrested, drunk on the street near his home in Albany.

She rarely heard from Justin and often forgot about him during the day. He would call, and she'd remember to worry again. If he stayed here, she wouldn't worry, but he wouldn't stay here, not for long.

"I'm not drinking," he told her. "You can't here. We take care of the dogs. It's supposed to teach us responsibility."

There were more than two dogs. He brought her to the back of the house and pointed through the window at the kennels in the backyard. At one end of the yard was a vegetable garden surrounded by a fence, and the grass looked trampled and brown in spots. Two men sat in chairs on the patio, smoking, watching the dogs staring at them from the kennels.

When they had time alone—well, not completely alone, as the two dogs slept on her feet while they sat at the kitchen table—Justin talked about his life here. He loved coming home to people and their ongoing business. She couldn't believe it. How could a person ever relax with all this blood pumping under one roof?

Later, they embraced at the door.

"I could come stay with you," he said. "Sometime soon."

"Of course you can," she said, but she was afraid of this thin, sad person in her arms. It would be a long time before they saw each other again.

Part One

BROTHER & SISTER

O ut of her scrubs, Willa examined herself in the bathroom. On her upper thigh, she discovered a vague hand-shaped mark from where a patient named Mr. Friedkin had slapped her. How the blood rushes to the skin like it wants to get out! Willa had just finished cleaning one of the sores on his leg when he hit her. An accident, he said. A reflex. But she was certain that he enjoyed remembering the feeling of his hand striking her. She was kicking herself now that she'd let him get away with it. True, he was an old man, but when she looked at the red mark on her thigh, she burned.

After her shower, she dripped around the apartment and landed on the futon. Explosion sounds rose up from the TV downstairs in Mrs. Flores's apartment. On the coffee table, her phone *mrrrr*d. A text from her brother. Justin's first transmission in a long time, almost a year.

Half my building collapsed.

It had to be a lie. She put the phone down by her leg. It continued to make noise.

I have no home. I'm on a bench in the park wrapped in a coat. A man gave me fifty cents.

She heard katydids sawing in the trees, as if she were in the park with him. She'd never visited him in Albany. She lived in New Paltz, a few towns over from their childhood home in Locust, almost two hours from Albany. She'd never wanted to leave Locust. Many of her high school classmates had left, moved to Manhattan or California or the south. She didn't blame them. There weren't many jobs here and the winters were brutal and sunless. In New Paltz, students from the nearby college took over during the school year. During the summer, cars lined Main Street heading to the Shawangunk Campgrounds and the Mohonk Preserve. Willa lived on a quiet street, far enough away from Main Street that she couldn't hear the bands playing in the bars.

Can I come? Justin texted. *I have nowhere to go.*

But it had been too long, and she didn't know him anymore. She wanted to be happy and free of his pain. He would find someone else if she never answered. She put on her robe and stood in front of the refrigerator and ate almost an entire bag of cherries, leaving behind bloody pits. Afterward, she closed herself in the workroom and sat at her desk while her stomach decided what it wanted to do with all the cherry meat.

At her desk she looked inside her latest diorama. Inside the box, she and Justin floated in impossibly blue water. Public pool water. You looked into it from the top, like a god. Hello, little things. The figures were naked. They were meant to be young, underage, before you were allowed to have a body. This moment at the pool had really happened.

She remembered it this way: he'd woken her some night when they were still friends and they'd walked in the dark to the Locust Village Park, hopping the fence to the pool. Justin removed his clothes. She must have averted her eyes, but remembered Justin, a mere mortal, soft and plump at the time, with hair on his tummy. That night, she'd surprised herself by going over the fence with him. Dead frogs littered the bottom of the pool.

A cherry burp surprised her. She placed tiny paper leaves on the water's surface with tweezers. A simple piece with little going on. Anyone but her would see nothing meaningful. So she'd failed, but continued to work on it anyway.

• •

When Luke arrived, she helped him out of his clothes and put him on the futon. She liked to roll the condom on and for him to watch her do it. She climbed on top of him.

They had met three months ago, at a bar "animal people" went to. That's how her best friend, Jenny, described it. Luke was a vet student, like Jenny. Large animal clinic. A group of sturdy people took up five seats at a table, with Willa among them. Earlier that day, the students had gone to look at a cow with a small window in its side, so they could see its digestive organs. Luke told her all about it and kissed her in the parking lot while she smoked a cigarette she'd stolen off someone else's table.

Luke's body was solid and nice to touch and squeeze. But he was losing his hair and wore glasses that didn't suit his face. He had a perfect past. He spoke about his brothers and sisters as if they were all friends. Instead of driving, he often ran to her apartment and jumped in her shower first thing.

As she orgasmed, she braced herself by putting her hands on his shoulders. Afterward, he disposed of the condom and dressed, too square to lie around naked. Nothing about his personality drew her to him, but she liked his body and the sex. Eventually, she'd know what to do about him.

"Maybe next time we'll make it to the bed," Luke said.

As a kid, he'd possessed beautiful dirty blond curls, which had fled when he reached twenty. He'd told her this the first night they met, after he'd taken off his baseball cap.

"Not the next time," she said. "But the time after that."

He laughed. He didn't act disappointed, or worried, so she didn't ask if he planned on leaving right away. Before him, there'd been Kevin, a house paint salesman who'd hung around for six months, but she found him slippery, never available when she wanted him. Kevin hadn't been cruel, but he wasn't nice, either. Luke was nice. She never imagined "niceness" would endear someone to her.

She rested on the futon with her robe underneath her until someone knocked on the door and she was forced to put it on again. Justin couldn't have arrived so suddenly, but here he was, looking like a dug-up tree root. Her brother. She hugged him quickly, and it felt real, not obligatory. His body heat radiated under his clothes and he was bony and unfamiliar. Something about the person he'd become repelled her. He was older, thirty-four, but he felt like her younger brother. He must have been fighting. There was a cut healing on his lip and a yellowish tone to his cheek. She wanted to ask who had hurt him, but he obviously didn't want to be asked questions.

"You smell like pond water," she said.

Justin pointed to the man on the couch. "Who's that?"

"Hurry, get in," Willa said.

"I'm Luke," Luke said, and held his hand out.

Justin let it hang there for too long, so Luke withdrew it.

"This is my brother," Willa said. "I'm sorry I forgot to tell you he was coming."

"She forgot to invite me, too," Justin said. He gently kicked a crate filled with odds and ends on the floor. "You turned into a pack rat."

"Not really," she said. Unpacked boxes slumped next to the TV. Justin kept rubbing a weird crusty stain on the leg of his jeans. His fingernails were filthy. He sat on the futon next to Luke. It was as if Justin had fallen through the roof and landed here, covered in plaster dust. She hurried into the bedroom and changed, hyperventilating as she pulled on a T-shirt and pajama pants. It took forever to put on clothes, and she'd left Justin and Luke alone together. When she entered the living room again, she wiped sweat from her upper lip.

"I haven't been sleeping," Justin told them.

"At all?" Luke asked.

"I must have at some point," Justin said.

"Otherwise you'd be dead," Luke said.

The skin around Justin's eyes was red; he'd rubbed at

them too much, and when he spoke, Willa smelled a familiar scent, a relative of the stink of manure from the fields by their childhood home. He didn't take care of himself. As a kid, he had primped in the mirror in a way that she never had. She hoped he didn't sense that she had just had sex right in the spot he was sitting. Luke's face showed nothing but interest in Justin. No shame or embarrassment. She sat on the floor between Luke's legs.

"Who is this guy?" Justin said. "Who exactly is this gentleman?"

"You know who he is," Willa said. "He told you."

"Does he need to be here?"

"I can leave if you want," Luke said.

"I don't want you to leave," Willa said, and rubbed his calf.

"I would appreciate it," Justin said.

"What is your problem?" Willa struggled to her feet.

"I think Willa wants me to stay," Luke said. "You want a drink or something?"

Justin's eyes rolled, exposing the whites, and she was afraid he might be having a seizure. "Do you need a buffer with me, Willa? I have important things to talk to you about, and I would prefer not to have an audience with spectacles."

Luke didn't react. Justin stared at him, leaned back on the futon, and closed his eyes.

"You know who dresses like that? Unassuming psycho-paths," Justin said. "One day, this guy is going to be caught decapitating little girls or something."

"You're a disaster." Willa stood in front of him and

kicked his shoe so he would pay attention to her instead of Luke.

"It was a real pleasure," Luke said.

She followed him out of the apartment and down the stairs, and he didn't speak again until they were in the street by his car. He leaned on it and crossed his arms. "That was interesting."

"I'm sorry," she said.

"Do you need help?" He glanced at the house.

"What? No. Of course not. I'll call you. Just wait for me to call you."

He got into the car without touching her, started the engine, and drove away. She stood watching the car go, and waited for a while.

"What did you say to him?" Justin asked when she came through the door. She hated that the weaker he got, the more she wanted to kick his ass.

"I said you wouldn't be here long," Willa said. "You didn't matter. You're not a real part of my life."

"I'll apologize to him."

"You won't have the opportunity." She sat on the futon.

"Is it so wrong I want to be alone with you after not seeing you for so long?" Justin said. "Then you show up with this guy who I don't know."

"You showed up. Why are you here?" Her legs and back ached. She spread out to find some relief.

"I told you. My building collapsed."

"Oh, come on."

"You don't believe me? You think nothing bad can ever

happen to me again? I'm telling the truth. It was on the news."

She kept silent so long, he shook the leg of her pajama pants.

"I have to get up really early," she said.

"Did Mom ask about me?"

"No," she said. So tired now, her throat went numb. Or it was the mention of their mother. They never talked about her without fighting.

"You didn't mean I don't matter. I am a part of your life."

"You are," she said.

She turned to face the back of the futon, the rope of sleep pulling at her head. She dreamed about him sliding out from under her legs and going off to find a safe place to sleep.

• •

The next morning, when she cleaned a young man's port through which poison medicine flowed, Willa pictured Justin's thin body, a picked-clean skeleton on her bedroom floor. Before she left that morning, he had woken up briefly. His hand rested on the pillow next to his battered face. Crosshatched abrasions decorated his knuckles and a brown crust lined his cuticles and nails. A semicircle scar interrupted the growth of his hair and glimmered when she turned on the lamp. Hi there. It smiled at her because they knew each other. All these years later, she didn't know exactly how he'd come by the scar.

When she was finished cleaning the young man's port,

she went to her next patient to check her vitals, waking the woman, who stared at her, trying to place her. The woman was recovering from a mastectomy. Willa checked her drainage, pale yellow with a thread of pink. Fine. The woman asked her questions she couldn't answer about her surgery, about her oncologist. The woman was on morphine. Willa took her temperature and it was slightly elevated.

Willa wasn't overly kind to the patients, but she wasn't mean or brusque with them, either. She tried to be serene, but her face appeared cruel even when she was feeling content or accomplished.

The woman tried to smile.

"You're looking really good," Willa told her.

She hoped Justin would stay inside today. She didn't want him to frighten Mrs. Flores. Mrs. Flores owned the house and lived loudly on the first floor. Willa never worried about her. She slammed doors and watched cop shows with the volume up. But if Justin was going to stay, Willa would have to tell her about him. She sensed Mrs. Flores would meet Justin and see Willa in a different light, see her as a certain type of person. Someone who might be trouble in the future.

The day Willa had viewed the apartment, Mrs. Flores took her by the hand and showed her the newly renovated bathroom. Her husband, she said, had designed it six months before he died. Willa didn't care much for the color of the tile, but she told Mrs. Flores it was beautiful.

"You don't smoke, do you?" she'd asked Willa.

"No."

"Oh good. I prefer a nonsmoker."

Mrs. Flores's clothes smelled of baked-in smoke that melded with her perfume. Burning flowers. Willa often came home and found the apartment stinking like the ghosts of cigarettes past. She imagined a giant set of lungs, the size of an apartment building.

At the nurses' station, she sat at a computer, where she spent too much of her shift. All of the information about her patients, the care she had provided, which she had checked off on charts, she now entered into the computer. The redundancy of the task drove her insane. She was constantly filling out paperwork, taking notes, checking boxes, entering data, often repeating the same information on several forms and in several databases.

• •

After her shift, she drove over to her mother's. She hadn't decided whether or not to tell Grace that Justin had come. Her mother lived in an old building in the small nearby town of Rosendale. The building was sandwiched between an abandoned factory and a rehabilitation facility for old people.

Sitting down in the kitchen, she refused anything except black coffee, which her mother always had brewing. Grace drank two cups in the morning, one in the afternoon, and one after dinner. She was in the middle of her evening cup. She brought it to the table, along with one for Willa. She looked tired and rumpled, like someone who hadn't left the house in a while. Willa tried not to show her shock: Grace was getting old. She was elderly. The skin of her neck crinkled and looked fragile, her eyes perpetually bloodshot.

"We should go shopping," Willa said. "Get some new clothes, maybe."

"Everything I have is fine," Grace said. About five years ago, she had sold their old house in Locust along with all their furniture, all the knickknacks, and the wingback chair she had treated like a museum piece. All through Willa and Justin's childhood, she had cleaned the living room every day. At the end of the night before she went to bed, the house looked like no one lived there. It used to drive Justin crazy. He was afraid to leave a fingerprint on the coffee table.

Grace furnished the new apartment with pieces from yard sales and cheap stores. The cups and saucers were mismatched and so were the kitchen chairs. She hadn't put blinds or shades on the living room windows. It was hard for Willa to witness her descent into someone who didn't care about keeping the kitchen or bathroom clean, didn't care about home comforts. Willa kept promising to help her, but never got around to doing it. Grace had never needed her help before. Willa wasn't sure how to do it.

Grace babbled about nothing, about what she'd cooked for dinner. How difficult it was to cook for one person. She'd bought beautiful summer squash, she told Willa, and had sautéed it. Ate it with rice. As she talked, she tore a napkin into confetti. Willa wished for something to happen. An object in the apartment below crashed and one of the kids cried.

Grace rolled her eyes. "They are the most misbehaved

children I've ever known in my life," she said. "Their mother is a druggy whore and their father smokes so much marijuana I practically ate all the food in the fridge before I realized what was happening to me. It drifts right through the floor." Grace sipped her coffee and a drop fell on her salmon-colored shirt. She brushed at it, which did nothing. She reached across the table and nudged Willa's arm.

"When you both were little, you both were lovely. Well behaved. Later, I don't know what happened. Not you. You were sweet and quiet. He would get out of control. Remember, he would hurt you? He pulled your arm out of its socket."

Grace didn't use Justin's name anymore. Willa decided not to tell her that he'd come. It would be a whole thing. Justin and Grace had never gotten along.

Downstairs, furniture scraped along the floor.

"I really should get blinds for these windows," she said, and brushed at the coffee stain on her shirt again. They moved into the living room to sit in front of the TV.

Justin hadn't pulled Willa's arm out of its socket. He'd pulled her too hard and she'd overextended the muscle in her shoulder, but it hadn't dislocated. Her mother had brutalized the memory, maybe not purposefully. Willa didn't correct her. Not now. Otherwise, they would argue and Grace would insist that her memory was the truth.

On her fifteenth July Fourth, Willa stood at the front window of their childhood home and watched Justin hold a Roman candle to his crotch and ejaculate comets of green and blue fire into the sky. He wagged his tongue at her and she gave him the finger. It had been raining for weeks. She thought she heard the fire sizzling out as it rose into the air. All the trees bowed around Justin, heavy with rain, and the flowers in the yard had developed white mildew.

When Justin came into the house with the smell of explosions on him, their mother eyed him from the couch. He crossed and stood at the sink to fill a glass.

"You must be very proud," Grace said. "You managed to get through it without blowing up your hand. Fireworks are for the mentally deficient."

Back in the living room, Willa looked down at the book she'd been reading since the summer started. It was called *Goodbye, Captain!* She had read the same two chapters over and over. In the book, a girl lives with her pilot father and poet mother in a little house in Queens, New York. She witnesses her mother receiving the news of a plane crash. How could a story go on from there when that was the worst thing

19

that could happen? Her ninth-grade English teacher had given her the book after their father died.

"I like fireworks," Justin said.

"It's embarrassing," Grace said.

Willa launched the book across the room, where it hit the small stand with her mother's favorite spider plant perched on top. Luckily, the stand only wobbled. She couldn't listen to another fight between her brother and her mother. Their fights started this way every time, with little comments that sounded like nothing, but the air around them lit up with tension.

Her mother stared down at the book Willa had thrown as if she could pick it up with her mind. She looked tired. She had gotten home from work, cooked dinner, and cleaned up. Willa had helped her with the dishes only after being asked a few times. "What the hell are you doing? Was that meant to hit me, Willa?"

"I'm sick of you two fighting," Willa said.

"We're not fighting," her mother said.

"In another minute you will be," Willa said.

On the inside of the book, her teacher had written: *Dear Willa, May you find comfort in this book, or at least a kindred spirit*. She hadn't. The girl in the story loved her mother too much and had no brother. Willa suspected the remaining chapters were about the girl being sad. Throwing the book had stopped Justin and Grace in their tracks. But now she had to go retrieve it; the cover had been bent completely in half.

Justin drank some of the water in his glass and emptied

the rest into the sink. His hands were blackened. Grace took the glass from him and tucked a chunk of his hair behind his ear. He had recently shaved one half of his hair off. Their mother took every opportunity to touch it and show her confusion.

Justin went into his room. Soon, crusty guitar and heavy drums vibrated through the house. Grace increased the volume on the TV until the announcer's voice distorted. On TV: a report about a volcanic eruption in another part of the world. The sky filled with black. In the corner of the screen, a shot from a satellite showing menacing smoke smeared across the ocean. Grace picked up a towel from the pile next to her and folded it into a perfect rectangle.

Willa sat in the comfy chair with her bent book in her lap and watched her mother trying to drown out Justin's music. She looked older than she had only a few months ago and was allowing the gray to come out in her hair. She'd never have done that while their father was alive. Soon, she'd be turning fifty, and Willa wondered if they should do something special for her but couldn't think of anything except cake. Her and Justin and a cake. It didn't sound special.

Their mother had changed the most since their father died. She'd never been sweet and nurturing, but when Arthur was alive, the two of them had acted as parents together in a way that made her softer.

A towel flopped over Willa's hands and the book. Her mother had thrown it.

"Some help would be appreciated," she said.

Willa got up from the chair and took a few more. She'd

fold them even though later her mother would shake them open again and refold them anyway. Before their father died, Grace had been just as obsessive, a cleaner and a stickler, but she'd gotten much worse. Willa would clean her room, make her bed, vacuum, then leave and stand in the hallway while her mother entered, remade the bed, and inspected the rest. Willa rolled her eyes at this, sometimes laughed at the insanity, but Justin didn't find it funny. If their mother tried to remake his bed, he screamed at her. He couldn't let it go.

She watched her mother now as she took the towels Willa had folded and undid them. She didn't even wait to do it until after Willa had left the room. *Refold all the towels you want*, Willa wanted to say, *he's still dead.*

• •

The next day, the sun appeared in the sky. Willa sat in the yard in a lawn chair with her sketchpad, trying to draw the oaks. They were too flat. She couldn't give them the weight they had in real life. That was the hard thing about drawing.

Justin climbed out the attic window and spread his body on the roof. He wore only a pair of briefs. The attic window like an eye behind him. He gleamed. Sea creature skin. Their mother was not home. Willa imagined Justin slipping off the roof and splattering his brains on the broken driveway. Their father would be mortified if he were alive to see his half-naked son on the roof.

She went to the top of the house and put her head out

the attic window. Heat radiated off the black roof shingles. She smelled Justin cooking in the air. He turned over on the towel. "Don't come out," he said. "You'll fall and I'll have to live with the guilt of killing you for the rest of my life."

"Get in here, dumbass."

"You don't care about looking like raw bread dough, but I do."

He turned away and put his hands behind his head. A few feet away, a wasp nest bulged out from the eaves, filled with thin black-and-yellow bodies. One crawled out of its cell and zoomed across her vision. Willa pulled herself inside and locked the window.

• •

That night, Justin lay naked and burnt on his bed. He wept. "Help me," he said. "Jesus fucking Christ." Willa heard him first. Then their mother came running into the room.

"He was on the roof," Willa said. She put her hand over her mouth. It had slipped out. She tried not to notice his naked butt. He must have taken his underwear off at some point. It was as red as the rest of him. When he'd tried to get back into the house and found the window locked, he'd called and called for her, like a dumb, giant bird. She listened to him for a while, trying to be mean, the way he was with her, but eventually she went up to let him in.

"On the roof?" Grace said. "Naked?"

"No!" Justin said. "She's lying."

"What do you mean, no? I can see your bright red ass

for myself." Grace sat on the edge of the bed and handled his body, examining him.

He shrieked. His skin looked bloody.

"Mom, stop it, please stop," Willa said.

"What a terrible thing you've done to yourself," Grace said. Her voice had softened, the anger fizzing out. "I'm sorry you're in so much pain, but it's your fault."

His only audience had been some blackbirds hanging out in the trees. None of their neighbors had witnessed his nakedness, as far as Willa knew. But she'd sold him out to their mother so quickly. Somehow, she'd have to ask his forgiveness.

Willa ran into the kitchen and took frozen aloe leaves out of the freezer and brought them to her mother. The leaves had fallen off the giant plant that had lived by the front window since the beginning of Willa's memories. Grace snapped one in two and slathered the yellowish juice on her fingers and painted Justin with it. To escape his screams, Willa ran from the room.

Later, she sat on the floor among Justin's clothes. Their mother was sleeping.

"You don't have to stay with me," he said.

Willa tanned but never burned. Her mother said it was because she'd inherited Sicilian skin from distant relatives who worked on boats and pulled octopi out of the sea. Justin had inherited their father's English skin. Arthur's family tree stretched back to Puritans, they were often told, as if that was something to be proud of.

"I'm going to puke," Justin said.

Willa jumped to her feet to get out of his path. Instead of rushing to the bathroom, he raised his head off the pillow, locked eyes with her, and emptied his guts onto the carpet.

• •

The next week, his skin started to peel off in white strips. Willa found it discarded here and there. He left it for her. She saw him unwrapping it off his back in front of the bathroom mirror.

"Help me," he said. He wore boxer shorts and nothing else. The bathroom smelled of the coconut-scented lotion he'd been using.

No. She didn't want to. Where he'd removed the skin, a pale pink, vaguely shiny flesh appeared. His face polished and new. A model of Justin.

"If you're not going to help, go away."

She remembered how he had cried and begged for help. She remembered selling him out. "Fine," she said, and chose a flake of skin on the center of his back that begged to be pulled. It detached easily and floated to the floor.

Justin laughed. "You'll do anything," he said.

• •

She had once loved Justin too much. Crushed on him. She hated to think about it. If only she'd been too young to remember, but it must have been when she was seven or so. It was obvious, too. "You're getting older," her mother said.

"You can't flirt with everyone anymore. Especially Justin. I never imagined I'd have to explain this to you."

"I know that!" Willa said. But no, it hadn't occurred to her that she should love her brother in a specific way.

She remembered wanting to learn how to be alone, to not need him. She walked in the fields behind the house, at the edge of the woods. She lay in the grass for a long time, long enough that she saw herself lying there, and she was no longer a human being. A katydid helicoptered onto her arm and didn't realize it had landed on a person. When she'd gotten back to the house, her body loose and her mind in the grass, her mother jolted her awake and held her by the arm.

"Are you insane?" her mother said.

Willa examined herself. Covered in grass and seeds and ticks, which her mother picked off one by one until she gave up and ordered Willa out of her clothes. They stood on the patio in the backyard and Willa stripped as slowly as possible.

"Hurry up," her mother said. "What do you think, the rabbits are taking pictures?"

• •

Willa lay on Jenny's bed with her feet on the slanting wall of Jenny's attic bedroom. They had done this, wasting hours, since they met in the sixth grade. Four years later, Jenny's bedroom had changed only slightly. She'd hung posters on the wall. PJ Harvey smiled crookedly at Willa with her red mouth, and curls of incense smoke floated to the ceiling.

Jenny dressed like a farm girl, not like the punk girls at school, who would have nothing to do with her, though she listened to the same music they did. Today she wore jean shorts and an oversized T-shirt that almost covered them.

Since Justin had gotten burned, Willa decided to spend more time away from home. She'd seen too much of him. When they were alone together in the house, the image of his writhing red body on his bed came back to her and repulsed her. They were around each other too often. He spent so much time almost naked now, and his body was changing, and he smelled bad. She told Jenny all of this. Told her about his sunburn and his shedding skin, and his underwear, the funk he left behind after coming in from the heat.

"I'm glad I don't have a brother," Jenny said. She sat on the carpet picking off candle wax. "Honestly, men disgust me. Including my father. I'm glad I don't have a sister, too, actually. I like having all the attention."

Jenny lit candles and incense and burned pieces of paper when they had nothing else to do. Willa worried she would burn the whole house down and there would be no more beautiful place to come to after school. She opened the window and let the smoke out.

The dog was coming up the stairs, the sound of tennis balls bouncing. He scratched at the door to be let in. Jenny got to her feet and opened the door and the dog hurried to the bed to bathe Willa's face with his tongue. She let him, briefly.

Jenny shut the door again. "Get off," she said, and pulled the dog off the bed.

"If I were your sister, you'd like it," Willa said.

"We probably wouldn't be friends."

"I'd wear your clothes without asking," Willa said.

They went downstairs and left the house. The dog barked at them. If they let him out, he would follow them into town. He complained from the window as they got onto Jenny's bike. Willa didn't have a bike. At first, she'd been afraid to get on the back of Jenny's, to stand on the pegs and hold on to Jenny's shoulders. She'd been afraid of falling off and cracking her head open, and more afraid of people from school seeing. The muscled shoulders inside Jenny's T-shirt rolled under Willa's hands. So unlike her own soft, nonexistent shoulders. Being around Jenny made her want to be strong, too, but she didn't have the knowledge required to get there. Her own family were horizontal people. Her mother rested when she got home from work. It didn't occur to her to take a walk or get into aerobics or yoga. She spent her energy on cleaning and collapsed after in front of the TV. Arthur, before his death, had once been fit. She'd seen pictures. The father she remembered had been plump, unable to hide a beer belly under his uniform. Justin had started using weights recently, but she suspected his motives were based on vanity rather than health.

It was a cloudy, humid day, and it had rained. When they got to the bridge and the small park at the edge of the creek there was no one else around. From her fanny pack, Jenny pulled two travel-sized mouthwash bottles filled with a pale golden liquid. When Willa unscrewed the cap and took a sip, she smelled clover and tasted honey with a bite.

"My dad made this out of honey from our bees," Jenny said. "It's his new thing."

"Does he know you have it?"

"Of course not."

"Oh," Willa said. "Good."

"Do you think they let me do anything I want?"

"Sometimes," Willa said, and they laughed.

By the time the small bottle was empty, the top of her head had flipped open and her brain hovered. She and Jenny walked to the edge of the creek, which was moving quickly from the earlier rain. Willa tripped on a piece of shale and frightened a heron neither one of them had noticed nearby, and it took off like a prehistoric bird. She put her arms around Jenny, pretending to be surprised, out of control, and too drunk to stand on her own.

Justin woke up confused. He was not in his own home, he was in Willa's apartment. The place where they grew up was a ten-minute drive from here. Too close. He lay on his side, facing the gray-and-yellow comforter hanging over the bed. A small nest of Willa's brown hair, a tumbleweed the size of a golf ball, fled into the darkness under the bed when he exhaled. He hadn't allowed himself to get into her bed last night. Willa had fallen asleep on the futon. He went into her room, put his bag on the floor, and slept with it tucked into his belly.

Earlier, when it was dark, he heard her come in and get changed, heard her moving around in the apartment, smelled coffee. Before leaving, she'd stopped to stare at him and he'd opened his eyes, but they hadn't spoken to each other. It was quiet now.

Around noon, he went into the kitchen to search for something to eat. Last night the place had appeared cluttered, messy. Now, with the sun coming through the windows, it looked like a nice place, nicer than any apartment he'd ever lived in, with enough room for a small dining table next to the kitchen. A vase of flowers stood in the center of the table. He hadn't noticed it last night. Maybe that guy had brought them to her, if men still did that. Willa hadn't completely unpacked. Crates of junk sat here and there, pushed against the wall and out of the way.

The cold refrigerator air roused him a bit. A glass pitcher of water magnified a bowl of grapes behind it, but when he grabbed the pitcher it slipped out of his hands and shattered on the floor by his bare feet. Icy water bathed his toes. He stepped away from it and onto the dry carpet in the living room.

He sat on the futon and watched stupid daytime crap on TV. A show with a panel of women talking about the news and celebrities. He knew nothing about either. On another show, a chef showed a petite woman in a coral-colored blazer how to make a grilled cheese, as if that needed to be taught. He didn't have a television at home. A person could sit and watch TV for hours and not think about it. A person could decide to only do that, and TV wasn't good for him. He should be challenging himself at all times, challenging his mind and memory. Making things, reading things. This was a time to start over now, with nothing. Willa didn't believe him about his building collapsing. All he needed was a computer to show her the proof, but he didn't see one around.

Earlier, he'd noticed the closed door next to the kitchen and assumed it was a closet. When he opened it, he saw familiar miniatures among the clutter, objects Willa had been collecting since she was a kid. Little bristle Christmas trees that she had bought at a craft shop. They'd once sat on the dresser in her childhood bedroom. No computer here, either. She must have hidden it from him on purpose, thinking he'd steal from her. He didn't need her fucking computer and didn't want anything from her he could stuff into his bag and take with him. Not any object, no money. And nowhere to put anything anyway.

This kind of disorder appealed to him. Obviously, an artist worked here. Piles of paper with sketches on them, books, and reminders towered on her desk. Their mother wouldn't have been able to rest in a house with a room like this.

He turned away from the scraps, pieces of wood, color swatches, paint jars and tubes, and found himself staring at scenes. So many of them, they appeared as a senseless jumble of figures and colors. Willa had stacked the wooden boxes on top of each other, as if she didn't care about them after she'd finished with them. Justin liked seeing them together, piled against the wall. The hours, days, months that she'd put into making them, and she'd tossed them aside. Many were unfinished. It didn't surprise him that Willa would quit on a project if it didn't work immediately.

On the desk he found a disorder of brushes with tiny bristles and jars of paint. A light on an adjustable arm, and a magnifying glass also attached to an adjustable arm hovered over one of Willa's projects. Inside the box on the desk a boy and girl floated in a pool.

When Willa got home from her mother's apartment, she noticed the workroom door was open. Things had been moved. She hadn't told him not to go in there, so it was her own fault. Why did she feel she had to hide what mattered to her from him? Because he might ruin it? She'd continue to make the dioramas after he went away again. If he disintegrated in front of her eyes, she'd continue. Broken glass gleamed on the kitchen floor. Justin sat on the futon with several of her boxes on the coffee table. She turned and threw her bag onto the floor, sending pens, a small bottle of hand sanitizer, her phone spilling out of the top.

"Jesus." She walked into the kitchen to investigate the broken glass. Drop a giant water pitcher and leave it for someone else to take care of. Why would a person leave broken glass all over the floor?

He put his hand on top of one of the dioramas.

"You never told me you did this."

"Why would I have told you?"

"This is an interesting fact about you."

"You never asked me," she said. "You never ask about me at all."

"You angry we don't know each other as well as we should?" Justin said. "Whose fault is that? If I didn't text you, I'd never hear from you again, I bet."

She took the dustpan from under the sink and made clattering noises.

"I'm sorry about the pitcher," he said.

"You couldn't pick up the glass?"

She plucked the big shards out first and set them aside on top of each other. She watched him carefully move the dioramas away from himself, to the other end of the coffee table. They were some of her larger ones. Inside the biggest, she'd built a replica of Justin's bedroom, as it had been right before he left. Almost empty, with a mattress on the floor. She'd never gotten around to putting his posters and books inside it. The tiny books would take a long time to make; she wanted them to be actual books with tiny pages. But Justin was there, standing by the window. In another, two young men stood by a bright red puddle. At the lip of the puddle, a girl in a snorkel mask peered into it.

"I like them," he said. "I can't believe you made them with your own two hands."

"You don't have to talk about it," she said.

"That guy is Nick, right? The girl and the boy are you and me. Why are you in them with me and Nick? You never met Nick."

Willa had never heard him say Nick's name aloud. It froze the air between them.

"It's not you," she said. "It's not me, either."

"A lot of these are my memories. Not yours," Justin said.

She abandoned the glass and as she rose from her crouch, her knees cracked. They were not his memories. They were tales. Some were inspired by him, she had to admit that.

"So now I'm not supposed to remember my life?" she said.

"You're a witness," Justin said.

She crossed her arms over her breasts and crushed them, the way their mother did whenever they argued. "Fuck, you're self-obsessed," she said. "They're not about you because you never told me anything. I was just supposed to take care of you and shut up and not ask questions."

He continued to inspect the objects in front of him as if he hadn't heard her. He wouldn't leave if she asked him to. She'd have to get someone to throw him out. The police!

I'm not a witness. From where she squatted, she saw a miniature version of herself looking out from one of the dioramas. A woman with a flashlight pointed at the ground. In a yellow circle of light, a man's head detached from a body.

• •

Justin went into the bathroom. Willa heard the water running for too long. When he came out, his hair was wet and slicked back and water dribbled down the front of his shirt. He made childish decisions. He'd washed his face and soaked himself in the process.

"Don't be angry at me," he said.

"I'm allowed to be a little angry," she said.

"I'm so tired. I don't think I've slept the way I did last

night in a long time. I want to do it again right now. Watch TV with me and make fun of it until I fall asleep."

"Is that what you did today?"

"Yes. I missed it."

Willa turned on the TV. When he fell asleep, she would have to see Luke. It had been weighing on her that he had driven away, and they hadn't spoken or texted. She hadn't told Jenny that Justin was back. Jenny would want to come over and help somehow.

"This show is terrible," Willa said, stopping on a sitcom about three men living with their best friend, a girl.

"Are those men straight?" Justin asked.

"Yes," Willa said. "I think so."

"And they all live with this girl and help her with her romance problems."

"Have you seen it before?"

"No."

"That's the show in a nutshell," Willa said.

When they were kids, they had watched TV together this way, making fun of older comedies that had not aged well. They'd liked surreal cartoons, nature documentaries, and shows about murder and detectives. Willa enjoyed guessing who the murderer was, but Justin never wanted to know, and Willa respected this and kept it to herself.

J ustin had started hiding in the library during his lunch
period, at a table by the window and a turning rack of
paperback classics. Three boys entered the library and sat
at the table with him. Their faces and shimmering jerseys
were familiar, but he had never said a word to them, though
they'd said plenty to him. One of them pulled a paper cup
from his pack and placed it on the table with a little *pock*
sound. One of the others brought something brown, like
a clump of mulch, to his mouth and placed it on the inside
of his cheek. The other two did the same, and they went
on talking quietly as they did it. Wet cigarette stink. They
passed the cup around and spat into it. The boys were mag-
netized to him. The more he wished to repel them, the closer
they came. Their lives didn't interest him, boys' lives and
interests. What were they doing, sucking on brown shit and
spitting into a cup? What was the appeal?

   The way they styled their hair, the clothes they wore,
and how they talked to each other, all of it disgusted him.
He didn't want them, though he imagined they thought he
must. Not at all. Many girls in his grade loved them and had
been used by them. How they breezed through life. How

they were other people's trouble. His trouble. To not be a boy, to not be one of them, would be a gift, and he wished for it at night, dreamed about it. Not to be a girl, but to be nothing.

"I know this guy," the one named Matt said. His slick hair would shatter if Justin brought a hammer to it. Crack through the shell and into the cream. At his hairline, red pimples sprouted. He spat into the cup and passed it to his neighbor.

"Me too," said the neighbor. A shadow of dark spit filled the paper cup. "He's all right."

"Does this bother you?" the one named Sean asked. "You don't mind if we do this here?"

"He doesn't care. You don't care, right?"

"No," Justin said. He closed his book, which was called *Lightning*, and put it in his bag. You could look at boys and want what you saw, the new muscle and hair, but you could hate them at the same time. A shitty feeling, similar to hating yourself.

"Bye, buddy," Matt said.

The bell hadn't rung, but the librarian didn't notice Justin leaving. He didn't cause disturbances at school. At the end of a long hall, he came to the metal double doors that opened into the gym, his next class. He tried to be early, to undress in peace before the others arrived. He didn't mind sports, but he preferred to exercise alone, without an audience. The locker room stank of something beyond what boys produced. He imagined mushrooms growing into the shapes of boys, out of sight.

He changed quickly and shoved his bag into the locker. As he tied his sneakers, the door opened and slammed shut. Someone walked to the showers and urinated and the sound rang out. When Justin walked around the row of lockers, someone grabbed his arm and pulled him back. Matt dropped him to the concrete floor and Kyle and Sean hurried to pin him. They didn't laugh.

Matt held the cup from the library with the spit inside.

"Do you swallow?" he said.

Matt squatted next to his head and squeezed his jaw. His mouth popped open and couldn't close and a creaky pain radiated to his ears. Saliva pooled in the back of his throat. Matt poured the contents of the cup into Justin's mouth. The paper touched his bottom lip. He tried to shake his head or turn away, but Matt wouldn't release his head.

Did Justin swallow? Nick never asked him to. Justin had no opinion or preference, but when Nick groaned, he took him out of his mouth and watched, wanting to see what he'd done to him. The sudden straining, the pump or the gush.

When the bitterness from inside the cup hit his tongue, the bell rang and they released him. He turned over and puked on the front of himself, his limbs bloodless and useless. The rest of the class entered the locker room. He got himself onto the bench nearby, but other boys stopped to gawk at him and grimace at the vomit on his shirt. He couldn't go out and pretend nothing had happened. He couldn't go out and tell. He walked out of the locker room and crossed the shining floors, heading to the door that led to the athletics fields.

"Where are you going, Dunham?" Mr. Correa shouted from somewhere behind him.

Justin ran, afraid Mr. Correa would come out and try to stop him. He hurried over the baseball diamond and kept going until he reached the fence and surprised himself by climbing over it without a fall.

In the woods, he took his shirt off to escape the smell, then lost it in the grass and bushes. His legs were wet up to the knees. His warm clothes were back in his gym locker. As he walked he crushed acorns from the shedding oaks. He didn't know he was going to Nick's until he came out of the trees and stepped onto Route 22. When the first car passed him, it slowed, and the driver, an older woman, peered out at him. She hesitated and vaguely urged the car toward the side of the road, but when he turned his head to it, she sped away.

Justin stopped at Nick's door and put his face up to the little window. Nick sat at his desk in front of his computer, doing whatever work he did to make money. Even on a cold day, he wore nothing but his underwear. On the floor around his chair lay a discarded blanket.

Nick answered the door with his blanket around himself, avoiding Justin's eyes. He searched the field and the road, as if worried that Justin had been followed. No one had seen him, only the lady in the car. Nick's arm appeared from under the blanket and pulled him in. The warm air in the apartment hit him and he fell onto the couch to shake. Did he have some disease now? Was he poisoned? He shivered with concentration. Nick put the blanket around him and disappeared into another room. Justin drooled and cried on the blanket. Nick reappeared and sat with him, pulled him close, and wiped his chin roughly.

"What happened?"

"Nothing. Nothing."

"You're freezing!"

In the bathroom, Justin took off his jeans and sat in the tub. Nick let the hot water fill it almost to the brim, and Justin couldn't move without some of the water spilling out. Nick's soap smelled too masculine, too blue. He squatted next to the tub and washed Justin's face until his forehead and cheeks burned. The smell overpowered him. He was used to the soap his mother bought, white or pink, the scent of wildflowers. A pain wobbled around inside his head from the soap's perfume. Justin pooled water in his hands and splashed it at his face.

Nick's soapy hands slid under the water and washed his feet and legs, and Justin laughed at his own big feet in Nick's hands like he'd caught two fish. No one had ever held his feet before. It was a weird feeling. Nick acted much older, but they were both kids. He was only twenty, three years older than Justin, but Justin felt far behind.

When the tub completely drained, he stood and Nick dried him with a towel.

"I can do that," Justin said.

"I'm helping," Nick said. The towel didn't smell clean. It smelled of Nick's skin, but Justin didn't want to be ungrateful.

• •

Justin wore one of Nick's large shirts and sat on the couch. Nick set some kind of grassy tea in front of him, but it tasted too bitter to drink. It came back to him now that he'd have to go to school tomorrow and see those boys. He'd forgotten. Being in Nick's place was like being in another dimension. Outside, it had gotten dark.

Nick offered him a boiled egg, a protein shake, half an avocado, a cracker. Nothing good. Nothing sugary. Justin's stomach whined and squirted boiling acid into his throat.

"You going to tell me what happened?"

"No."

A phone rang and rang on Nick's desk. It went silent and started again. Nick rose from the chair, unclicked the cord from the jack, joined Justin on the couch and pulled him close. Justin allowed it, but he didn't feel soothed tonight. Justin's penis grew hard under the blanket on his lap and Nick reached underneath and put his hand around it and held it without moving. Semen gushed out of Justin, with little sensation. Nick removed the blanket.

"Jesus, I hardly touched you," Nick said. He rose from the couch and disappeared into the bathroom, returning with toilet paper. Justin cleaned himself and handed the paper back to Nick. His body was doing things beyond his control. He needed to be unconscious.

He fell in and out of sleep, waking to Nick's mouth on his, and his hand rubbing him until his body turned warm and unbearable. He twisted away and curled up on the other side of the couch. Nick never sensed what Justin wanted at any specific time. When Justin wanted his attention, he couldn't get it, and when he wanted a little space, Nick didn't give it.

"You better tell me what happened right now," Nick said, close to his ear.

But if he opened his mouth, whatever came out would not have the weight of what happened to him. It would be small. Just words. Nick wouldn't feel the terror.

• •

When Justin walked through the door, his mother was waiting for him. He'd hoped she'd be in bed and he'd coast through without her seeing him in Nick's clothes.

"What are you wearing?" Grace said.

Willa stayed in her room, her crappy music tinkling out from under the door. One of Grace's favorite cop shows played on the TV.

"Those are not your clothes."

"My friend gave them to me."

"What friend? Why would you need your friend's clothes?" The TV light animated her body. "I don't want to know. I don't want to know about your life. Maybe it's better I don't."

"I had a bad day," he said.

"I can only imagine what you've been up to," Grace said. "What happened to your clothes, Justin?"

"They got messed up."

"Go to bed."

At some earlier time, he might have wanted to collapse

at her feet and beg her to put her arms around him, but he'd grown accustomed to not needing her. When he'd been too young to know any better, he used to try.

He stopped at Willa's door and knocked on it. She opened it without comment and let him in. They didn't speak. He sat on the floor and played deejay, sliding CDs into the player, trying to keep the mood in the room level. Willa lay on the bed doing her homework, closed a textbook, and opened her sketch pad, which he had never seen inside.

"Where were you?" she said. "I waited for you."

"I told you not to."

He had no friends. She'd been his only friend for a long time, and he often resisted it. But not tonight.

• •

After school the next day, he walked to Nick's through the woods again, like a crazy person. Hunters were out. No one had bothered him today, and when he saw the boys, it was as if they'd never met him. He kept quiet, and his mind listed possibilities. None of it had happened; the boys never touched him.

At Nick's, he knocked on the door and waited. Nick would be home. He worked early in the morning at the gym and came home to work on his computer. Justin tapped on the window. The curtains hung open, and Nick sat at the desk, again with his blanket wrapped around him. On the computer screen were boxes of text ticking upward as Nick typed. Chatting. Nick clicked the mouse and a picture slowly appeared. A man's naked body.

Why wouldn't he answer? Justin sat against the front door. A couple of guys from one of the other apartments clomped down the steps and passed him, not noticing. The other night, what had he said that made Nick angry? Nothing. He'd barely said a word. He had pushed Nick away from him when Nick tried to start something. If he just opened the door now, they'd talk and Justin could let him know that he did want him. Needed him, actually. Had nothing else. But more than needing him, he wanted him, which is more important and better than needing someone. He thought this about Willa, but only when they weren't together. He didn't appreciate someone if they were standing next to him.

He struggled out of his crouching position, the seat of his jeans cold from the concrete. His knuckles split as he hammered at the door. On the walk home, he licked the blood. Other animals moved in the dark, safe now that the sun had set. He stumbled into some bushes. Most had thorns and tore at his cheeks.

Willa walked into the "animal people" bar, which was really called Devon's, to meet Jenny and Luke. A greenish light hung over the tables. A row of booths lined the wall to her left, and the old wooden floor rose and dipped in places. Most of the patrons were older, owners of nearby farms. Jenny sat at a booth with the same group she was always with.

"It's the nurse," a woman said, looking up at Willa.

Jenny slid out of the booth and hugged her. She wore jean shorts and a tank top, men's work boots. She smelled like beer. Willa never doubted Jenny's love, but Jenny didn't often embrace Willa with abandon, not unless they'd both been drinking. As kids, they'd slept in the same bed or had fallen asleep in Jenny's living room by the woodstove with some part of their bodies touching.

"Luke's here," Jenny said.

"I know," Willa said. "He texted me to come."

"Oh, is that why you're here? I thought you just appeared because I was bored with these nerds."

Willa pulled a chair from a nearby table and sat at the end of the booth. Luke glanced at her from his corner. There were two people between them. They couldn't talk here. She smiled at him and he smiled back but said nothing.

"What can I get you?" Jenny asked.

"I can't drink. I'm not staying long."

"Because of him?" Jenny said. She gestured at Luke with her head. "I should never have introduced you to him. I don't know him that well. He's probably terrible. Why is he just sitting there?"

Willa hoped none of the others heard this. Jenny would feel bad about it tomorrow. She worked with these people and cared about them, otherwise Willa wouldn't have been allowed in their presence.

"No. Not him," Willa said. "Justin's here."

Jenny glanced over Willa's head. "Not here?"

"He's at the apartment," Willa said. "I hate that he's there all day by himself. He's sleeping now. I don't know what's wrong with him or what he wants me to do about it. The last I knew he was doing okay, working, and he had his own place. He showed up the other night when I was with Luke, and he acted like such an asshole."

"If you don't talk about someone, they cease to exist," Jenny said, drunkenly.

"I talk about him."

"This is the first I'm hearing his name in a long time. You don't want him here. You should get him help."

Whenever Willa talked about Justin, she felt she was betraying him, and it would bring her bad luck.

"I could come over," Jenny said. "If you need backup."

"No. I'm just venting."

Jenny rubbed Willa's hand. Someone put Dolly Parton on the jukebox, and Jenny laughed, delighted. Willa and Jenny both loved Dolly Parton. Whoever had chosen the song, "Coat of Many Colors," must have been an interesting person. It wasn't a bar song.

"He's mad at me," Willa said. "For what, I don't know."

"Shhh," Jenny said. "Listen."

• •

Luke escaped the booth and bent to whisper in her ear. He smelled of beer and his strong cedar deodorant.

"Come with me."

Willa followed him and turned back once. Jenny's eyebrows danced. Outside, the night had cooled, but the humidity wet her bare arms and legs. Mosquitoes landed on her and stuck. She got into Luke's cramped car, which smelled dusty and faintly of cow manure.

"Neither one of us did anything wrong," Luke said.

"Right," Willa said.

"You didn't expect me to sit there and be insulted by your brother, did you?"

"Of course not."

"And I'm not blaming you," he said.

"He's not a bad person," Willa said. "He made a bad impression." She didn't feel right saying more about Justin, making excuses for him, but she didn't like hearing someone else say that Justin had behaved badly. She used the excuse for him that she had when they were younger, though it turned her stomach. "He has a brain injury. He had an accident when he was a kid. I don't know if that matters or why I'm telling you. It's not an excuse. He recovered well, and honestly he was always kind of a jerk."

"I'm sorry," Luke said. "You don't have to explain."

"He's had it rough. I don't know what else to say."

"Don't say any more," Luke said.

Out the window, dark fields rushed by. They were near Locust now, but heading away from it in the direction of the dairy farms, corn, and soy fields a few towns over. Was this nice person going to murder her and leave her in a field for cows to discover? Insects, attracted to the headlights, flew into the windshield and left smears.

"Where are you taking me?" Willa asked.

"My parents' house," Luke said.

"I know where you grew up. It's not that different from where I did."

"This is the perfect time," he said.

Soon, he pulled the car over and they walked on a long, quiet road. It was nearly midnight, and there were no lights or cars. The moon partially lit the field to the left of them, but she couldn't see the cows he insisted were there. She'd been wrong, she hadn't grown up in a place like this. She'd lived in a neighborhood, with other houses nearby.

"It would be nice to stay out here for a long time," Willa said. She meant alone. To be alone in the dark and the wet warmth, to close her eyes and be a blob of flesh. She expected him to reach out and take her hand, surprise her with a kiss. She imagined them fucking on the road in the dark. Instead, they walked side by side without touching or talking.

Luke stopped walking.

"Hello?" he said.

At first, she thought it was a person coming upon them. A cat trotted between their legs holding something in its mouth.

"What have you got?" Luke said, bending to examine the cat. "It's a flying squirrel."

"What? Seriously?" Willa said.

Luke shone his cell phone light on the cat, a smooth striped creature with large, deep black pupils. Night eyes. It dropped the animal from its mouth. An animal that would be at home in South America more than upstate New York. Tiny, exotic thing with big ears and flaps of gray fur-covered flesh under its arms. Luke stroked the dead squirrel's head with his finger.

"You murderer," he said to the cat.

Willa wanted to touch Luke. She placed her hand on the back of his neck and he turned to look back at the dead squirrel, a disappointed noise in his throat.

Willa came home from work with gifts, and Justin accepted them though it embarrassed him. A bottle of body wash and his own shampoo, a grooming kit in a small case. There were new clothes folded next to these items. A pair of sweatpants, socks, T-shirts, stiff new jeans. She'd bought him a package of underwear.

"Jeez, Willa," he said. "I can buy my own underwear."

"You need it, right?"

"Yes. Thank you. You didn't have to do that."

He took it all into the bathroom. Under a hot shower he squeezed the body wash onto his chest and rubbed it into a lather over his neck. After, he clipped his finger- and toenails and pumped some of Willa's hair spray onto his hand and ran it through his hair. He unwound too much floss and went at his teeth, but his gums bled so profusely he couldn't bring himself to finish the job. Blood specks on the porcelain sink disturbed him.

• •

Willa took him to her favorite places in town. They walked off her street and onto a busy strip with bars, a pizza place, music stores, and antique shops.

They stopped at a bookstore she thought he'd like. She was excited to show him. She kept touching his sleeve, so he would follow her to another section, another wall of discolored paperbacks. He didn't have any money with him, so he didn't take anything off the shelves, afraid she might insist on buying it for him. He mourned his books back in Albany. And before that, his small collection of fantasy and science fiction novels that he had allowed Grace to donate when she sold the house in Locust. He wanted to buy books and keep them, though he often couldn't get through reading them.

"Do you have a lot of books?" Willa asked.

"I did."

• •

At a small, empty Thai restaurant, she ordered for him. As they sat, the lights faded to amber, signaling that it was the dinner shift. The waitress, who wore a long black braid, gave them water, and after five minutes brought out a plate of spring rolls they hadn't asked for. She knew Willa. The waitress gave him a knowing smile. She must have thought he and Willa were on a date. Soon, she brought out a bowl of noodles decorated with spring onions.

"This is the only good thing," Willa whispered. "But it's really good."

He twirled the noodles around his fork. They were

savory and nutty and hot. He was happy they were being kind to one another, though this wouldn't be their lives, this was a night out. When they got home, the feeling would cease. They ate quietly for so long, he forced himself to break the silence. "How's your friend?" he said. "The guy."

He couldn't remember how, though it was only a few days ago, but he understood that he had acted badly to her friend.

"He's fine," she said. "Eat more."

"I'm full," he told her.

"Justin, I can't eat all of this myself."

He pulled more noodles onto his plate. A pop song in another language played. Willa paid the check without making a fuss and Justin looked at the art on the walls. Big framed photos of women in traditional costumes. Bright colors and beautiful women.

On the street again, the drinkers were out. Rough boys with their rough dogs sat on the curb in front of a coffee shop. Willa and Justin stepped around them.

"I have money," he told her. "In the bank."

"Okay," she said.

"Not a lot, but I have some. I lost my ATM card, but I can get my money. I can give you some."

"I don't want any."

He desperately wanted to pay her back, but for now he had nothing in his pocket except his empty wallet. If she kept giving him things, she would resent him.

• •

Justin didn't tell Willa that before he'd come to New Paltz, he'd seen Nick around Albany. She would say, *No, you didn't. You imagined it.* Nick was long gone. In jail or dead.

Justin had been living in Albany for a year before he spotted Nick. He'd grown accustomed to living alone, going to work, walking through the park and watching people. He visited a coffee shop most mornings and bought a buttered roll and milky coffee, which he took on the bus with him. He lived in an old building with problems, cracks in the walls, rustling and scratching sounds, but it was cheap enough that he didn't need roommates. The landlord lived far away and wanted tenants he didn't have to worry about.

In the park, Justin sat on one of the green hills and watched dogs and their owners. Once in a while, a dog would find him, come near and sniff. If he was lucky, one would approach him fearlessly and ask for affection, and he would caress its head and hold its paw until its owner called it away. He couldn't care for himself, so he couldn't care for a dog either. Brief encounters with other people's dogs fulfilled him. Almost.

He worked in a supermarket deli for part of the day, and after took the bus to the mall to cashier at an electronics store. After his shift at the supermarket, he removed his red polo and pulled on a blue one. The black pants and sneakers worked for both jobs. By the time he arrived home at eleven, his feet were sore, and he barely had the strength to shower.

One day in the spring, he saw Nick from the bus, right before the Washington Park stop on Madison Avenue, so he got off, though it would make him late for his job at the supermarket, and he followed him. He noticed beautiful men, but no longer desired them. Well, that wasn't exactly true. The desire arrived but fear killed it. He tracked Nick into the park, across the park road, and onto the gravel path around the lake, which smelled of rot. A group of little boys threw bread at the mallards and Justin almost told them to stop. Bread was terrible for ducks. Junk food.

Nick wore fashionable jeans that hugged his thick legs. It was the body that drew Justin in. Nick had grown a full beard and had put on weight. Justin wanted to push him into the water. It would only be embarrassing, not dangerous. Nick couldn't possibly be here, in Albany of all places. Fifteen or more years had passed. It wasn't Nick.

Are you? he wanted to say. Instead, Justin walked by, knocked some of his hair over the side of his face, but it didn't matter. The man, Nick, didn't notice him.

The next day, Nick came into the grocery store. Justin had never seen him there before. He must have just arrived in town.

When he came to the deli counter to order, Justin's heart withered, but he wasn't afraid of being recognized, as he looked nothing like he had at sixteen or seventeen. He was only afraid of being this close, speaking to Nick again. *You shouldn't be allowed to go to grocery stores. You shouldn't be allowed to exist.* His hands shook with anger as he sliced turkey and handed the thin bag to Nick over the counter, and Nick took it from him as if it were nothing.

After Nick left, Justin asked to take a break. He hated having to ask to leave the deli counter, ask to go to the bathroom. He grabbed his backpack and went out behind the supermarket and leaned against the building. He'd been trying to read through a copy of *The Marble Faun* that he'd found in a cardboard free box on Lark Street. He was having trouble getting past the first few chapters; though he enjoyed the writing, he found it hard to keep track of the characters. It frustrated him and frightened him. He would get better if he read more and worked on his memory. Often, after work, he'd drink at a bar and stumble home to sleep. He hadn't been treating himself kindly.

"I shall be content, then," rejoined Miriam, "if I could only forget one day of all my life."

At home, after he'd let his guard down, relaxed under a hot shower, he sat on his bed naked and suffered an attack of intense fear. What if he had been followed home? Of course, he hadn't. He was safe. No one would hurt him. For the previous year, he'd felt foolishly safe in this apartment on the third floor.

His spirit floated out of the top of his head. His throat swelled. He inhaled with such force, he barked trying to get air into his lungs. To pull himself out of whatever this was, he burst from his position and closed the door to his bedroom, thinking it would make him feel secure. When it didn't, he tried to trick his body. His muscles cramped, and his heart squeezed his blood. He would die here. He punched at the lamp on his end table and shattered it like a thick-shelled egg and cut his knuckles. The shock of what he'd done, the broken pieces at his feet, brought him back, and he sat on the bed again, exhausted.

J ustin came out of school and saw Nick's car parked across
the street, his arm draped out the driver's side window.
A bus pulled up to the curb and blocked the car, and Justin
was grateful. No one would be paying attention to him as he
hurried into the car.

"I thought you were done with me," he said as he slid
onto the passenger seat.

"Why would you think that?"

"You didn't answer the door when I came over the other
night."

"When did you come over?" Nick asked.

"You know when. I knocked. On the door and the window." The car smelled meaty. Nick's body produced the
smell, smoky and bloody. He sucked on mints and wore po-
made in his hair, and the scent of these spiked through the
other. He didn't call himself gay.

"Shit, you look so sad," Nick said. "Even sadder than
before. Are you crying?"

"I'm not crying," Justin said. "I don't care." It was more
attractive to be unharmed.

Nick started the engine. "Sure you don't."

"Why'd you come here?"

"Maybe you can show me the guys who hurt you."

The car idled, heat puffing from the vents, the windows open. No one noticed. Justin made sure by watching students come out of the building, talking, lighting cigarettes, and turning to go one way or another. Willa appeared and zipped her jacket to her neck. She looked seriously dorky. He wasn't popular, but he managed not to dress like it.

"You tell me when you see them." Nick slipped his aviators out of his front pocket and slid them on. He put effort into being manly.

"I don't want to," Justin said. "I shouldn't have told you. You'll make it worse."

"Why won't you let me help you?" Nick said.

"Quit pretending you care."

"You're the most important person in my life. Why do you think I'm here?"

The most important? What would be expected of him, the most important person? He'd dreamed about someone needing him, loving him. Justin put his hand over Nick's thick fingers, which rested on the gearshift, and a warm ribbon tightened around his middle, which must have been something close to love.

• •

They played video games together. The kind where you were a soldier, but all you saw was a gun pointing at things. Nick wore only his underwear. When he exploded someone or something, or when blood spurted, his toes flexed against the carpet. They watched movies or porn, but Justin didn't want to watch porn with Nick. He didn't need help to get aroused. All he had to do was look at Nick and he was ready. Nick's ears aroused him, his nose, his eyebrows, his hairy calves. When he was happy, he worried about the day he would not have Nick. If he screwed up somehow and lost him, he would never be lucky enough to have someone like Nick again.

"You're dying, bitch," Nick said.

"I don't care. I'm not good at this."

"If you leave me to die, you're in big trouble."

"What kind of trouble?" Justin said. "What will you do to me?" He stood in front of the TV. Behind him Nick's character grunted in pain.

Nick set his controller on the couch cushion. "Do you want to watch me work out?"

"Okay," Justin said, though he hadn't expected this. What should he do with his face? When he sat, he tucked his hands under his thighs. Nick went to the weight machine against the wall and faced Justin with his legs spread wide, then pulled the cords, and the weights rose and fell behind him. His body tightened, and blood traveled into his face. His forehead gleamed. He exhaled a controlled, hissing breath. The machine shimmied as if its screws were coming loose.

"Do you like this?" Nick asked.

"I . . . guess," Justin said, and laughed a little.

Nick let the weights return to starting position and he stood. The veins in his arms embarrassed Justin.

"What's funny?"

"Nothing. I just—"

"Don't laugh at me. Do you know how much work this takes?"

"I saw," Justin said. "You work really hard."

"You're a smartass," Nick said. "Get on the floor and take my dick out."

Justin wanted to laugh. That was his first instinct when it came to anything considered sexy. After the fear. At school, he'd learned that if you had sex with men, you got AIDS. The fear didn't keep him from coming here. He wanted Nick more than he feared becoming one of the men he'd seen on TV, wasted down to skeletons.

To the right of them, the front window shimmered as the sun set. Nick hadn't closed the curtains. Anyone could see in. Justin closed his eyes but saw the window in his mind. He sensed someone watching.

"Should you put a condom on it?" Justin said. He'd asked before, and they used one when they had sex. You got it from oral, too, didn't you?

"Shut up," Nick said. "You don't know anything."

"No," Justin said. "I don't."

"Do what I tell you to do and don't ask questions."

He didn't want to ask questions. He didn't want to speak ever again. It frightened him, the way his mind went blank with happiness when Nick's hands cradled his head to guide him. How could he think of putting a condom in his mouth? He loved the taste of Nick, the taste of salt on his tongue. He didn't ask if he was any good at this, afraid of the answer he'd get, but Nick moaned above him, his fingers curling in Justin's hair.

· ·

Justin lay in his own bed with a candle Nick had given him burning on the bedside table, filling the room with a scent similar to Nick's cologne. When Willa came to the door, he watched a cloud of the smell hit her in the face, and he waited for her to turn around and flee, but she didn't.

The candle made him think about burying his face in Nick's armpit or feeling Nick's weight crushing him into the bed. The first time they kissed, Nick had ground himself into Justin so hard that on the walk home, the muscles around Justin's waist and groin smarted. He'd cum in his underwear and hidden it from Nick, making some excuse to leave. In the woods, he'd quickly taken his shorts and underwear off, left the underwear on the ground, kicked dirt and dead pine needles over it, and pulled his shorts back on.

Willa shut the door behind her. Their mother was slamming pots and pans onto the stove, so they would know she was working without their help. The TV kept her company. Since their father died, Grace didn't like a quiet house, always wanted the TV or the radio playing. She couldn't be left alone for long, and soon would be calling Willa out to help her with dinner. She didn't bother Justin anymore. He pretended to have disappeared when she called him.

"Who was that?" Willa said. "In the car."

He'd looked right at her from Nick's car and swore she hadn't seen him.

"Is he your boyfriend?"

"No, Willa, jeez."

"I don't care," she said. "You don't have to hide it from me. How old is he?"

"Why? Do you think I'm being molested?"

"Whatever," she said. "Are you, though?"

"He's only a couple of years older, and no, I'm not being molested. It's none of your fucking business, and if you tell Mom anything, I will pretend you never existed. When I look at you, I'll see an empty seat."

"I'm not spying on you," she said. "You were right in front of the school. People saw you. I'm not the one you should worry about."

"You're Mom's little spy. You're a big eyeball."

Willa's eyes widened. "Fuck you."

"Just get out before she calls you." He couldn't stop himself. She shouldn't have mentioned Nick to him. He'd assumed he was invisible, and he'd been wrong. People saw. If she was trying to help, she'd done it the wrong way.

"By the way," Willa said. "It smells like ass in here."

• •

Grace invited Justin to take a ride with her, so she could talk to him, she said. Normally, he wouldn't have gone, but she'd been uncharacteristically serene. It caught him off guard. She didn't try to be overly sweet, but she spoke quietly, and when he passed her in the kitchen, she squeezed his shoulder.

They drove through the neighborhoods on the other side of the big orchard across from their development. Long streets with ranch-style houses and clipped lawns, kids on bikes, people walking their dogs. Her bracelet with multi-colored stones clicked against the steering wheel. When he was little, she'd allowed him to fasten it for her.

"I love this idea," she said, and turned the radio off. "Taking someone out in a car. You're trapped. So we can really have a good talk without you running away like you always do."

Outside the windows, fields of grayish dirt appeared. All the corn had been cut weeks ago. Deer grazed, looking for the left-behind cobs.

"Justin, you're becoming something I can't support," she said with gentle concern. "I can't put my finger on what it is, but I sense it in you. I wanted you to know this because I sometimes think you feel I'm angry at you for no reason, but this is the reason. Do you understand what I mean?"

He couldn't speak; otherwise he would cry in front of her, which he wouldn't give her. She didn't deserve to know how she'd hurt him. An invisible hand squeezed his throat. Later, maybe he'd tell Willa about this and she wouldn't believe him, and he would have to hate her.

Would she hurt him somehow, kill them both because she thought he was a demon? He felt a little out of tune or weird, but not rotten. Before this, he'd assumed she was disappointed because he was gay, but it was something more.

He turned his head and watched her drive the car. Nothing about the way she moved told him they were going to die today. She slowed the car, made a three-point turn, and headed back in the direction they'd come from. The back of his T-shirt stuck to his wet skin.

When he looked at her, she was a stranger, gripping the steering wheel, her nails polished but bitten past the nail beds, her cuticles raw and pink.

On a Saturday evening, while Willa prepared dinner, Justin came into her kitchen with his hair wet and pasted down from the shower. His skin was scrubbed clean. Drops of water fell from his beard and onto his shirt. He'd inherited their father's bone structure and a strong nose the rest of his features lived quietly around. The wound on his lip had healed. When he sat to put on his socks, she noticed several warts on the bottoms of his feet. They were covered over in pale, tough skin.

"You need a treatment for those," she said. "I'll pick something up for you."

"For what?"

"You have warts on the bottoms of your feet."

"I never look at the bottoms of my feet. Who does that?"

"The entire human race," she said.

The first few nights of his stay, pulled out of sleep by anxiety, she'd gotten out of bed during the night to check on him. Each time, she found him sleeping peacefully on the futon. Maybe sleep had been the answer all along. One of those nights, as she stood in her doorway, she heard something working either in the kitchen or somewhere behind the wall in the living room. The sound of little claws excavating. In the dark it worried her more than it would have in the light. This was an old house, full of mice or squirrels. They had probably chewed all the electrical wiring.

She had not asked him yet when he planned on going back to Albany, or if anyone was waiting for him to come back. He had a job at a grocery store. He never mentioned friends.

He insisted on helping her. She didn't want him touching her plates, which had belonged to their grandmother in New Hampshire. She gave him the job of setting out the napkins and cutlery. The rest of the time, he sat and watched her cook.

Luke arrived. He was late. Justin surprised her by answering the door and shaking Luke's hand, putting the other on Luke's shoulder. Tonight, he acted like the men in movies. The way men acted when they were together and had decided on friendship rather than war.

Luke wore cargo shorts and a loose-fitting T-shirt, and a baseball cap, which he removed. He smoothed his remaining hair. He didn't handle conflict well, he'd told her, had never been in a bar fight, had never gotten a black eye or broken a limb, not during his entire childhood living with an older brother. When she'd invited him, he told her he would start fresh with Justin.

On his way into the kitchen, Luke stopped to look at the diorama on the coffee table.

"Gosh," he said. He often said "gosh" when he was stumped. She'd begun to notice it, but tried not to count. She went to him and kissed him on the side of the mouth.

Justin had begged her to let him keep the diorama out.

It showed a girl and a small deer on a golden leash heading into a forest of black trees. The deer was smooth and tan, with little stubs for antlers. The girl wore overalls Willa had made out of a scrap of denim. They were walking, leaving behind them a figure on the ground, a young man with blood around his body. Justin's attraction to it panicked her, briefly. She'd built it, remembering the time he'd run away, when she'd imagined all the terrible things that must have been happening to him, when she'd wanted to know so much where he'd gone, she'd wished to be with him, a feeling that had surprised her at the time.

"Where'd this come from?" Luke said.

"Willa made it."

"I thought you painted or something," Luke said.

"Neat, right?" Justin said.

"It's really good, I think," Luke said.

"They're not all like that," she said.

"She's a real artist," Justin said. "She's always been an artist, but she hid it. You had to hide things in our house."

Willa placed her laptop on the coffee table and put on some music she'd curated specifically for this dinner, a playlist of classical pieces she'd chosen at random, with a few quiet songs she knew. When they sat down to dinner, Luke let the questions fly. The last time anyone had seen her work had been in art school, during the few semesters she'd attended. She'd never forgotten some of her critiques. Her classmates found her work easy, one-note, and precious.

"Did you ever think of showing them to anyone?" Luke said.

"Like who?"

"An art person?"

"I don't know any art people."

"Well," Justin said, and clapped his hands together. "Since you don't know any art people, they might as well stay in your closet forever."

In front of him, Justin's untouched food resembled a prop. She saw him eat one piece of broccoli.

"Sounds fine," she said.

"He's encouraging you," Luke said. "They're good." Now they were on the same team. Two men who would tell her what to do with her mediocrity.

"You've only seen one."

"You should see the rest of them," Justin said. "There's tons."

"Can we just eat dinner, please," she said. A roasted potato with one burnt side crackled in her mouth and bitterness coated her tongue.

"A lot of them are about me," Justin said. "So she's uncomfortable talking about it, because I'm here. If I weren't here, she might talk about it, or you might never know. You might never know about me, either."

"I see," Luke said.

"They are not all about you," she said.

A raucous piano piece started playing. A folk dance, with drums and tambourines, the piano played in a percussive style. It rubbed her nerves, but she didn't get up to change it.

"They're about our childhood," Justin told Luke.

"Oh yeah? What was Willa like?" Luke had eaten each section of his plate separately. First the broccoli, next the potatoes and the chicken. He ate the way someone who thinks about food as fuel eats. He'd left the crisp chicken skin uneaten.

Willa had barely gotten through her food. Over the last few years, she'd become conscious of the speed at which she consumed. She'd trained herself to eat slowly. When Justin spoke, she stopped cutting her chicken halfway through, and placed her silverware on the napkin.

"Willa was always sweet," Justin said. "I don't know where her good heart came from. Maybe my father, actually. He wasn't complete shit, not to her. I used to think, there's no way Willa's going to survive in the world."

Luke reached under the table and rubbed her leg with his fingertips, but she couldn't take her eyes off Justin. She didn't recognize the girl Justin described. Aren't all children a little afraid of the world? Doesn't it seem like they'll never survive? She had let her guard down after their night out together, and now she sensed a cruelty in the room. Justin wanted to hurt her, but maybe only when Luke was around.

"Willa's a nurse. She's healing people. Saving lives. I thought she'd end up in an eating disorder treatment facility," Justin said. "I'm surprised Mom didn't turn you into one of those girls. She almost did."

"Jesus Christ, Justin."

"It's a good thing," he said. "You're fine. Not like me."

"And what's wrong with you?" Luke said.

She detected a rare edge in Luke's voice, and she hooked herself to it. The skin on her arms and face sizzled. She would have killed for a glass of wine, but she had decided not to buy any. She'd never thought of Justin as an alcoholic, but he had a drinking problem, or did at one point. He had kept things from her, gave her just enough information. He couldn't afford rehab, but he had gone to meetings, he said. Before moving to Albany, he'd lived in a house with recovering addicts. They helped him do what was right for him, he said. Maybe he'd been drinking in Albany. Maybe he was on drugs right now.

Through the living room window, she saw the sky had turned an uncommon orange. Normally, she'd have taken a picture with her phone.

"What happened to your face?" Willa asked. "And your hand. Were you in a fight?"

"I don't want to talk about it in mixed company," Justin said.

Luke shifted in his chair. Willa thought she saw him glance at the front door.

"You talked about me," Willa said. "Now talk about yourself a little. I want to know what's going on with you since you invited yourself into my apartment."

"Don't fight," Luke said.

"I want to know," Willa said, her voice raising to half a yell.

"I'm a poltergeist," Justin said. "I apologize for my presence."

"You aren't a poltergeist," Luke said. "A poltergeist is caused by you."

"Never mind," Willa said. "Why don't we stop talking."

"Tell me more about when you and Willa were kids," Luke said.

"We were best friends," Justin said. "When we were really little. We had dance parties in Willa's bedroom."

"I was Justin's doll," Willa said.

"You were not," Justin said. "Grace always said that. 'She's not a toy, Justin!' I never thought you were."

Willa would not remind him that he had hurt her, that he had danced with her so hard, he had wrenched her arm. She didn't remember the pain. The memory of that had been erased.

"Did you have a happy life?" Justin asked. "A simple childhood? Did you have dogs growing up?"

Luke placed his crumpled napkin in the center of his plate.

"You don't want to know about me," Luke said. "You want to embarrass your sister."

"I want to hear about it," Willa said. "Did you have dogs?" The exuberant piano song ended. Cilla Black came on to sing "Anyone Who Had a Heart." What had she been thinking with this playlist?

"I do want to know about you," Justin said. He cut into his chicken and ate a few pieces. As Luke spoke, Justin ate with his head down, to show he wasn't interested.

"When I was a kid, my family owned an orchard," Luke said. "I had to work there in the summer and fall. People came to pick apples and I worked in the store. We did have dogs. My favorite was called Hutch. He was a pointer-retriever mix. He liked to run around the orchard and he'd bring back things people left; kids left toys, dolls and stuff. My brother would drive us through the orchard after dark in one of our golf carts and Hutch would lie in the back. I'd let him hold my arm in his mouth like a dead duck. It was sort of comforting. One night, we were out too late. It was too dark to be out on a cart. They didn't have headlights. My brother ran over something, maybe a pothole in one of the paths, and Hutch fell out the back of the cart. Anyway, he broke one of his front legs. I remember carrying him out of the orchard and he was howling." Luke laughed. "That can't be true. Maybe my brother carried him. But I remember doing it. I didn't speak to my brother for a week after that."

"You blamed him for breaking Hutch's leg?" Justin asked.

"Yes, I did," Luke said. "I think I was thirteen maybe. I completely blamed him. He still brings it up, that I made him feel so guilty when he already felt terrible."

"What happened to Hutch?" Willa asked. She imagined Luke, the thirteen-year-old version of him, which she had to invent in her mind, holding his dog's paw as the vet administered the lethal injection.

"Oh. Nothing. He was fine. He didn't need surgery or anything. Healed okay."

"Is that the worst thing that ever happened to you in your life?" Justin asked.

"Justin," Willa said. She hated the suggestion that Luke deserved to be mocked because he hadn't suffered.

"Of course not," Luke said. "You didn't ask to hear

about the worst thing that ever happened to me. I told you the first thing that came to mind. You asked if I had dogs. Yes, I did. Many."

"I know what I need to know about you now," Justin said.

The first time Justin saw Nick, he was a sophomore and Nick was a senior. Nick had beard-scruff when none of the other boys were able to grow any. He looked older and terrifying, the way beautiful things could be when you were not beautiful yourself.

Almost two years later, Justin saw him on his computer. He appeared, trapped in a little square on the screen, with a description below. It was a surprise to see him there, on a site for gay men. Justin had assumed he was straight. He assumed most of the boys at school were, unless they obviously weren't. Those boys he avoided, as they were too much like him, and together they would draw attention.

The description read: "My name is Nick A. I am twenty years old and work as a trainer. Interests: working out, hiking, video games, movies, and good music. (Good music = punk, hip-hop, some jazz. No fucking pop music. Don't talk to me about fucking house music.)"

A picture of his face and a picture of his body. Justin never expected to see his body on his computer screen. He certainly never expected to see it in real life, to touch it and pine for it.

• •

Nick picked him up at school and they drove into towns Justin had never been to and walked among strangers. Justin was getting used to going places without needing his mother to take him, without asking if he could go. He went where he wanted to now, because of Nick. He loved being in Nick's car. If they chose to drive around for hours without a destination, he'd be happy. They went to the Galleria Mall, fearless, though they didn't touch each other in view of anyone. People noticed Nick's handsome face, and it was like walking around with a celebrity. Justin felt more important, excited to be doing something simple. In a music store, Nick stroked Justin's arm as they browsed through CDs.

"You listen to her?" Nick said when Justin stopped to examine a Tori Amos CD.

"I like her voice," Justin said.

"I can't let you buy that faggy music," Nick said.

The word stung him. Justin put the CD back in its place.

"Do you really want it?" Nick said.

Justin shrugged.

"I'll steal it for you."

"I don't want it that bad," Justin said.

They didn't buy or steal anything. In the food court, they ordered lunch at China View, and when it was time to pay, Nick searched himself.

"I . . . forgot my wallet," he said. "Shit. I'm sorry."

Justin paid. He guessed it was only fair since Nick usually paid for things.

After lunch they ducked into a high-end clothing store and Nick picked out a pile of sweaters and jeans for Justin to try on, and they entered a dressing room together. Justin assumed there must be cameras watching. When he tried to undress himself, Nick stopped him and did it for him.

"You're too slow," he said, and helped Justin off with his sweatshirt.

The air in the cubicle was stifling. Nick placed his cool hands on Justin's chest and Justin recoiled at the difference in temperature, his nipples turning hard. Nick tweaked one and Justin yelped and hit him.

"Quit it!"

He grew so aroused he couldn't button the jeans he was trying on. Nick laughed and sat on the bench next to the mirror.

"You look good in everything," he said.

• •

On the way back to Locust they stopped at a pond, ten miles from town, and sat in the gravel and stared at the water, the sun setting over it. A sheet of yellow oval leaves lay over the water, shed by a nearby tree. Soon the pond would freeze, and they would come back and walk on it. In the summer, maybe they'd swim here together.

He enjoyed making out in the cool autumn air. To feel Nick's scalding tongue slide over his lips. But he was too scared to do anything else out in the open. There were people who lived near the pond.

"You can't live your life like that," Nick said. "Afraid. You're so timid. And you're weak." He held Justin's skinny arm. "The world is going to fuck with you. It already is. Do you think those guys would have done to me what they did to you? No. Because they'd know I'd kill them before they touched me. You make it easy for people to hurt you."

"Why are you being so mean?" Justin asked. Hearing these things from Nick hurt more than if his mother or Willa had said them. He only wanted Nick to be easy on him.

"This isn't mean," Nick said. "It's truth-telling, which is important and helps you. Especially when I'm trying to make you into something. You have to get harder or people will always take advantage of you."

They had their arms around each other. Nick placed Justin's hand on the hard bulge in his jeans.

"Take it out," he said.

"Can't we just go home?"

"Do it," Nick said. "You can't be afraid of taking chances."

"It's not that . . ."

"Jesus, forget it," Nick said, and removed Justin's hand from his crotch. He turned to face the water. Justin stared at him. How could he change so quickly? He was finished with Justin. After the day they had together, the shift cut Justin. He'd ruined their time.

"I'm sorry," he said. In his mind, he did what Nick wanted him to do, but it took his body another minute to try it in reality. He went for the buttons of Nick's jeans and undid the top one. When he tried to open the second, Nick stopped him and held his hands rather than pushing them away. "Okay," Nick said. "I get it. You tried."

• •

That evening, they shut themselves in Nick's bedroom. Justin didn't say it, but this was his favorite. Not watching TV or playing games. Getting into bed, turning the lights off, shedding clothes, being warm, sleeping, fucking around, talking. The shades drawn, the clock radio playing. He forgot what time it was or that he would have to go home at some point. He liked the way Nick loved his body, though it lacked specialness. It had no shape to it. But Nick took bites out of him and licked him from his armpits to his feet. It embarrassed and thrilled him. The more they were together and naked, the more he wanted to be, and wanted to leave home, never speak to his mother or Willa again. They no longer mattered.

When they weren't together, he lay on his bed with the candle Nick had given him burning on the night table. He let it burn for a few minutes before blowing it out, so it would last.

Nick wrapped his legs around him, and they were so strong Justin couldn't get out of their grip. He had never been this tired. Under the covers the air turned tropical. At home, his mother would be wondering where he was, why he hadn't been coming home right after school. He hated having to come up with lies, making up friends he didn't have.

"I have to go," Justin said. But Nick held him. His soft penis smooshed against Justin's thigh.

"I'll take you home," Nick said. "Talk to your mother. Show her how normal I am."

She didn't know about Nick, of course. Not the tiniest idea about him, because she would lose her mind. Grace would never dream him up. That someone like Nick would want her son.

"Are you crazy?" Justin said.

"She doesn't have to worry about me. Maybe you wouldn't have to think about getting home all the time."

"I'd still have to."

"She controls you," Nick said.

"I guess." Justin moved his body to show he wanted to get out of bed. "It's getting too hot."

"You can break the rules." Nick undid his legs, and cool air rushed at Justin's stomach and chest. "If you cared about me. I'm starting to think there's only one reason you come here."

But it wasn't true. If Justin tried to deny it, he'd sound like a liar. He put on his underwear and T-shirt. Nick turned over and slipped his hands behind his head on the pillow. A thread holding them together broke, and Justin hurried around to the other side of the bed to try and grab it back. Nick's eyes were rubber balls. Justin didn't see himself in them or anything else, no light or life. He grabbed Nick by the shoulders and shook him to try to make his eyes go back to the way they were.

"I love you!" Justin said. "I really, really do. Believe me."

Later, walking home, his ribs plinked and a cool mist circulated through him. He'd acted so stupid. Nick must have been embarrassed for him, because he got nice again and said goodbye, see you later, but didn't kiss Justin.

Justin had vacuumed Willa's apartment and cleaned the bathroom, and now sat on the floor in his underwear, overheated. The air conditioner struggled. Outside, the sun pummeled the roof. Willa had left for work when the light was pink. She obviously wanted him to go away, but he didn't want to leave, as much as he wasn't welcome. He'd been inappropriate. Telling secrets. Embarrassing her in front of Luke. If he stopped screwing up, losing his temper, she'd have an easier time getting used to the idea of him staying.

The neighbor downstairs turned the TV up and sound vibrated through the floor and into his ass. Justin rubbed himself through his underwear. He had not had an erection in weeks. Too busy, too preoccupied with being afraid. He pulled the band of his underwear down and let out his dick and put his hand around it to feel the warmth and foreign stiffness. He jerked it for a while. The light outside told him nothing. The passage of time didn't register, but it had been a long time. No pleasure. Nothing happened, and probably never would, though he kept trying until he hurt himself. If he couldn't have this one thing, if he wasn't allowed pleasure, what would it matter if he had a home or not? He hid his red self away in his underwear again.

In the kitchen, he flipped open the little address book next to the phone and tore a page out of it before thinking. To only have one person in the world is a dangerous thing.

• •

He walked a long way from where the bus left him, on a busy road with a supermarket and a Walmart. He stopped into a gas station to ask directions. The man behind the counter didn't know where Meadow Lane was, but Justin asked a woman who was pumping gas and she pointed at the road, in the direction he'd been walking. She had a black dot in the white of her right eye. It was large enough he saw it from where he stood, by the trunk of her car.

"Keep going that way," she said. "Not far."

The heat of the day intensified. After a half mile, he turned onto Meadow Lane, a gravel road with two apartment houses. Dust billowed around him. There had been no rain for two weeks.

Once he stopped walking, sweat raced out of him, dribbled down his back and into his underwear. His clothes were soggy and his mouth glued shut. Wild children, wild from summer and dirt-covered, surrounded him.

"Are you homeless?" a little girl asked.

"Yes," he said.

"Go away," one of the boys said. "I have a gun."

"You do?" Justin said.

"Our dad does," the girl said.

"Shut up!" Her brother shoved her so hard the girl stumbled to her left but managed to keep from falling.

She removed a mirror-faced phone from her pocket and snapped a picture of Justin.

"I'm going to show this to him right now." She ran off with her proof and her brothers followed, turning to sneer at him once before they disappeared into the house.

He took the paper out of his pocket. The right house, but no apartment number. Did his mother live with these children? Around the back of the house he found another door and peered into the small window at a staircase. Instead of knocking, he opened it and went up the stairs.

His mother opened the door after the first knock, as if she'd heard the ruckus outside and expected him. She'd lost weight and had let her hair go gray. When she saw him at first, she closed the door partway.

"What do you want?" she said.

Did she not recognize him? Or did she recognize him and not want him here? She held the door wide open and sized him up, as if she saw something in the rest of him, something aside from his face that told her who he was.

"Mom, it's Justin."

"I know that," she said, but he could tell she hadn't. "Come in."

He entered the apartment and she hugged him for longer than he'd anticipated. She cleared her throat and stepped away from him, her hand lingering on his arm. Sunlight settled on her simple furniture. The kind of place he felt comfortable in. A clean apartment that never truly got clean because it was too old. After a while, there was only so much you could do. The smell of old dust, linoleum, glue, mice, all of it permanent. It must drive her crazy, but he'd lived in similar places. She'd been a meticulous housekeeper during his childhood, didn't like to leave a single glass or fork in the sink.

"Sit," she said. "Sit at the table. You're soaked with sweat."

She placed a frosty glass of water in front of him. He took two gulps and the cold dribbled through his body, into his empty stomach. He put a cold hand on his forehead.

"I forgot to eat," he said.

"I didn't expect to see you," Grace said. "Does Willa know you're here?"

She stood at the counter. He saw himself through her eyes, a feeling he'd had many times as a kid. Whatever he was, he wasn't her son. Not only that, he was like someone who'd come to fix something in her apartment, someone she'd tolerate until whatever broken thing was fixed.

"No. Not here."

"Has she seen you?"

"I'm staying with her," he told her.

"I guess I shouldn't be surprised she didn't tell me. I wish I could say you look good. But you don't. You look terrible. Just terrible."

"I know."

Being near her frightened him. He wanted her to be kind, to go easy on him, but her coldness invaded him. She wanted him to be hurt. She turned away and filled a teapot and scraped it onto a coil on the stovetop.

"Do you need money?"

"No."

"Why are you here? After six years. Without a call to see how I am."

"I always ask," he said. "I ask Willa."

"She doesn't mention you."

"I ask," he said again. The muscles in his chest tightened. Grace didn't face him and smile. When she'd hugged him it had meant nothing, an automatic gesture.

A weeping fit attacked him, and he inhaled a bit of saliva, covered his face with his hands, and his body shuddered in the squeaky chair as he coughed and sobbed. His voice strained. He wanted to swallow it, the way he'd seen other men try to hide their tears. He'd witnessed this when he lived in a house with four other men, all recovering addicts, men with frightening faces, with scars, desperately trying to hold on to their masks. He lifted his head and took a napkin from the holder next to him to blow his nose.

"I know why you'd stay away," his mother said. "You could never take responsibility for anything. You're old enough now to learn from your mistakes and become a better person. Do you think of yourself, how you were, the kind of boy you were? You never wanted our help."

"I think about it."

She drew closer to the table and he saw real feeling in her eyes. Pity. He turned to the window. "You didn't have to be so desperate to defy me," she said. "You could have been a normal boy, but you tried so hard not to be."

"I don't want to talk about that. I didn't come here for that."

She sat across from him and folded her hands, the skin dangerously thin. She hadn't changed in any other way. She still looked like his mother, still acted like her, but her skin showed the years, gently sliding down from the bones of her face. When she lifted her arm, he saw she had no muscle. The flesh hung and if he touched it he knew it would be soft and empty. He hated the concern in her face. She thought he'd always been his own problem. He no longer wanted kindness from her; it had been foolish to come here, as if he hadn't known what would happen.

On the table, some of the condensation from the water glass traveled in a sparkling line from the base of the glass to the center of the table as he watched. He willed the water to move by imagining it, but in reality it stopped while the water in his mind continued. Maybe he didn't move it at all. He caught her watching him concentrating. He pictured the glass sliding gently off the edge of the table, but it didn't, so he helped it with his hand. It bounced on the linoleum and the ice cubes skidded across the floor.

Grace got out of her chair and bent to rescue the glass.

"You haven't grown up one bit," she said.

In Willa's front yard, next to the irises, a woman smoked. Justin watched her. She stood with a hose emptying into the garden, drowning the flowers. He was exhausted after talking to his mother. Bees fled the water and flew past his head.

"Are you the boyfriend?" said the woman.

"The brother," Justin said.

"That makes more sense."

She hurried to turn off the squeaky valve and the water ceased flooding the garden. The air smelled of iron and the perfume of the irises mingled with smoke. She glared at the cigarette in her hand, annoyed with it, and threw it into the mud.

"Your sister is lovely. She's the best tenant I've ever had." She waited for him to respond, and when he didn't, she told him: "You look sick."

"No," he said. "I'm fine." He put out his clammy hand to her and she shook it. "My name's Justin."

"I'm René," she said.

"I just remembered something," he said.

"What's that?"

"I don't have a key to get back into the apartment. I left without thinking about it. I went to go see my mother. I hadn't seen her in six years."

"Six years? How does a person stay away from their kid for six years?" René said.

"We don't know what to do with each other."

She opened the front door and went into the house and he hesitated to follow her. The sight of her trusting back worried him. She didn't turn once.

"I meant to say you can come in," she said.

The television chatted about grilling stone fruit. On the screen, a woman turned peaches over to expose where they'd been charred. He averted his eyes from the blackened yellow fruit.

"You shouldn't let men you don't know into your house," he said.

"I never imagined I'd be surrounded by so many sad children in my old age," she said. "This neighborhood is full of them. They all go to the college."

He sat on the couch, but first moved the plump pillows out of his way so he wouldn't crush them. Was he one of the sad children?

"They drink too much! Once, I found one of them in my living room. He was so drunk he thought this was his house. I've been here for twenty-five years and that was a first. This used to be a normal neighborhood with families."

Around him, objects looked as if they had never been moved or touched. She'd collected a trove of glass animals and colorful paperweights. Photos of family members hung on the walls, but she didn't appear in any of them. He was afraid he might break something. His head swirled. He'd left his mother's with the belief that he would never see her again, but before he walked out, she'd squeezed his arm and asked that they have dinner with Willa soon.

René sat in a chair across from the television. Her hair was dyed a dusty brown and the gray inched up from her scalp. She must have been in her late seventies, at least. The sun brought out freckles on her tanned face. The living room got a lot of sun, but it didn't cheer him. He had always liked people who created environments for themselves, like terrariums. On the shelves on the far wall were stacks of wrinkled mystery paperbacks, a row of succulents in varying stages of life and death. She should have a cat or a dog, but he didn't see evidence of a pet.

"I do have a spare key," she said, but didn't move to get it.

All the breakable things watched him.

• •

When Willa arrived home, he was gone. Justin had cleared the bedding off the futon. She sensed a release in the air, as if humidity had broken. Why would he go and not say anything? She searched for a note. Next to the phone, the address book lay open. Someone had torn a page from it. There were little squares of paper caught in the rings holding the book together. The page behind the torn-out one had dots of bled-through black marker on it from when she'd scribbled her mother's address.

She called Grace, and the phone rang and rang until a message played, telling her the person she'd dialed was not available. Her mother was the only person she knew who had an answering machine.

She found his bag behind the futon just as the phone rang. The bag smelled like Justin, a shrunken and concentrated version of him. She shoved it away from herself with her foot.

"You sound worried," Mrs. Flores said. "He didn't want me to call."

"He's down there?"

"He's watching the television now," she whispered. "He doesn't know I called you. He told me everything."

Everything? Willa took the phone to the table and sat.

"I know it's not my business," Mrs. Flores continued. "And I know siblings fight. My own children sometimes frightened me! The way people who should love each other can hurt one another. I was a social worker for years. Did you know that? Families can do horrible things to each other."

"Yes?" Willa said.

"He says you threw a water jug at him. That you slapped him. He doesn't feel welcome back. He's been wandering around since last night."

Willa laughed into the phone. She was sure Mrs. Flores had to pull the phone away from her ear.

"He told you I hit him?"

Mrs. Flores's lips popped as she took a drag from a cigarette.

"Yes," she said. "That's what he told me."

"Do you think I'd do something like that?"

"I don't know. Gentle people are capable of violence in private. I wouldn't have believed it if I didn't see for myself how he looks."

"Well, I didn't," Willa said. "He lied to you."

"I don't know anything about that," Mrs. Flores said. "I just know what I see. He's in danger. Either it's you or something else."

"I'm coming," Willa said.

In her scrubs, she looked sensible and trustworthy. She kept them on. It was the hottest part of the day, when the sun beat against the house. It blinded her as she went down the stairs. Flies had hatched and buzzed into the air from the trash cans and frenzied around her as she stepped onto the pavement. When Mrs. Flores opened the door, Willa saw Justin on the overstuffed couch, an empty plate on the table in front of him. Remnants of cigarette smoke curled in the air, and Mrs. Flores walked through it.

Willa sat next to Justin and Mrs. Flores left the room but hovered in the entryway of the kitchen with her arms crossed over her chest. Justin's battered hands rested between his legs. His clothes were rumpled, and he smelled as if he'd been running around in the heat.

"Tell me," she said.

"Tell you what?" he said.

"What's happening to you? I want to understand."

"You mean you don't already? What kind of nurse are you? You can't see inside me and I'm your brother. How can you help strangers?"

"I can't see inside anyone," she said. "But I think you need to check in with a doctor. I don't know how many years it's been, but obviously you're not taking care of yourself." Mrs. Flores had disappeared. "You told her I hit you. This is my home. I have to live here and now she thinks I hit you."

"The more I told her the nicer she was to me."

"Oh my god."

"I went to see Mom."

Her heart beat against the muscles of her chest. She didn't want to hear about their mother. She wanted her relationship with him to be an island, one Grace couldn't reach. That was impossible. But maybe not. Maybe it would simplify things.

"She didn't want to see me," he said. "She says you never mention me. She didn't know I was in town."

"I didn't know what to do."

"It's okay. I wouldn't have, either." He shifted to face her. "So I came here. I forgot the key. That's the only reason I'm here. I met René."

René? Mrs. Flores had never asked her to call her René. What was so special about Justin that he'd gained that privilege?

"Just tell me," she said, and she put her hands on top of his. "What do you need?"

He struggled to breathe. The warmth of his hands faded until they were cold stones. She rubbed them.

"Breathe slowly," she said.

"My building really did collapse."

She tried hard not to sigh in his face. She held her breath.

"I didn't lie about that. But part of me knew it was going to happen. There were little hints here and there. I'd walk into my place and think I'd seen something move. I'd be doing the dishes and a picture would fall off the wall. I was afraid someone was coming, maybe, or something would happen. And I'd panic. I thought I was dying."

"Come back upstairs," she said. "Please. We'll talk about this more. She doesn't need to hear all this."

"She said I can sleep here if you didn't have room for me."

"I have room. Please."

They rose from the couch together, and before they entered the kitchen, Mrs. Flores appeared. Justin touched her wrist with his ugly hand.

"Thank you, René," he said.

"Nice to have some company in the middle of the day," she said. "If you're staying, you can come and see me."

Willa expected him to accept this invitation right away.

"I want you to know I lied to you," he said. "Willa didn't hit me. She'd never do that."

Mrs. Flores put her hands in her pockets. Willa noticed mud splatter on her jeans.

"All right," Mrs. Flores said. Willa waited for her to continue, to apologize for believing that she'd hit Justin. She didn't speak again. She opened the door for them and they stood outside. Insects vibrated in the trees.

Justin came out of school, but Nick's car wasn't there. He waited for the traffic to die and the buses to leave. On the other side of the street, he leaned against the tree where Nick usually parked. After twenty minutes, Nick didn't show. He was late. Or gone. Justin's body turned cold. He'd been ditched.

The smokers huddled in a group nearby, sending a bluish cloud into the trees. They weren't allowed to smoke on the sidewalk in front of the school.

He walked, almost in a trance, to Nick's apartment. The lights were on inside. Nick's car sat in the gravel, but when Justin knocked Nick wouldn't answer.

"It's me," he yelled through the closed door.

He should break one of the windows. Take a stone from the garden and put it through the front window. Maybe Nick had gotten bored with him. Maybe it was over. He beat at the glass instead of throwing a rock, beating it with his fists until the front door opened. Nick hurried out and grabbed him by the arms and threw him into the grass.

"Can I have one night to myself?" he shouted.

"I thought you were going to be there," Justin said.

He heard the whine in his own voice and hated himself. He wanted to bury himself.

"This isn't good," Nick said. "You sound like a bitch."

Justin stood and brushed the ass of his jeans. "I'm sorry. Please don't hate me."

"Go home, Justin." Nick turned and went into the apartment. Justin would never knock on the door again and be sure he'd be let in.

His eyes filmed over on the walk home. The sun was already going down and the light in the woods turned brown. By an old tree, he collapsed and dug pale mushrooms out of the dirt and stuffed them into his mouth and chewed them into mud. They tasted like the smell of a field of manure.

• •

He could barely keep his hand steady to open the door. His mother hurried to him when she saw him. He allowed her to help him to the bathroom, but wanted her to go away once he was there. She wasn't comforting. She became angry when he or Willa got sick; she blamed them, though she did what she thought mothers should. Sat with them as they puked, fetched a washcloth to cool their foreheads. She stood in the doorway now and waited to see what was wrong with him.

"Go away," he warned her.

"Whatever you want," she said.

His organs leapt. He took off his clothes and sat on the toilet and let go of the poison inside him. Whatever it was burned on the way out. After, he stood under the shower for ages, and when he was done he walked dripping into his bedroom. Willa and his mother both witnessed it and screamed at him to cover himself. He locked the door and his mother knocked more than she usually did and soon gave up. A short time later, Willa's voice called to him.

"Are you okay? Justin?"

He slept and woke when the door opened. He had locked it, but it opened and in came his mother. He didn't have the strength to yell at her, so he turned his back to her and pulled the covers over himself. The bed springs creaked. Her hand landed on his back and rubbed.

"I've always had a key to this room," she told him. "How are you feeling?"

"Fine," he said.

"Where were you after school? What were you doing?"

"Nothing."

"I wish you were a nice boy who did normal things."

"I am. I do."

She stayed for a while, rubbing his back until he pretended to sleep. Once she left, he lit Nick's candle. Next to him, *My Antonia* lay open to the same page he'd been reading for days. Tomorrow in American Lit, they were having a discussion. He would be called on and would not know who the people in the book were or what they'd experienced.

He put on clothes and climbed out the window, landing on the patio. In the field behind the house, the evening deer spooked and bounded away from him. He turned his hands to claws and stalked them like a werewolf. A skunk ran away from him, its white back-fur visible in the grass. The air smelled of cold and burning tires. In the woods, he decided to freeze to death. He walked for a while and came to the little brook running over slabs of shale. If he put his hand in the water and into the bed, out came clumps of gray clay. He would lie in the brook.

He'd taken Nick here once and they hooked up. Under the cover of trees, he didn't worry. He'd put his hand around Nick's cock and loved the feeling of it growing against his palm. Nick's cum leapt into the water and rushed away from them.

• •

The next day, he didn't wait to see if Nick would arrive. He wanted to be alone if he couldn't be with Nick, so he hurried out of the school to avoid running into Willa and her friend Jenny. The sky was clear and the air cold. As he walked, he heard voices he recognized behind him. Matt and the other two guys, Kyle and Sean. He didn't need to turn around to know it.

They wouldn't hurt him out here in front of the world. People drove by. Other kids passed on foot or on bikes. He wanted to start running, cut across the front lawn of the school, into the back fields and the woods. But they might catch him there and do whatever they wanted to him. And no one would see. No one had seen what had happened to him in the locker room, so it hadn't happened.

"Where's your boyfriend?" Matt said.

"Justin, we're talking to you."

"He's pretending he can't hear us."

"Justin? Where's your daddy?"

My daddy is dead. They didn't know that, did they? Arthur. He'd gone through a period where he forgot his father had died. If he left the house for a long time and came back, he expected to see Arthur. He woke in the morning and forgot. I forgot Dad is dead.

Not that they ever got along well, or were ever comfortable around each other, but wouldn't it be better if he were alive? He would have taken care of this. There was something inside both of them that opposed the other, and nothing was ever easy between them. Willa loved Arthur. When they were kids, she'd leap into his arms like a pet monkey. When he died, she turned into the new Willa. He barely remembered the old one, except that they had fun together, conspired against their mother together. Not now, though.

"My dad is dead," he said out loud, but they didn't hear him.

"Your boyfriend, faggot," one of them said. "He's waiting for you in front of school."

No, he almost said. *Not anymore.*

At the end of the street, he turned right onto a long quiet road with old trees on both sides. The boys remained behind, never getting closer. Most students took the bus or walked along the main roads. He chose the tree-muffled quiet. A car pulled next to him and the window squealed down. He kept walking. The boys wouldn't touch him. They were enjoying torturing him. The car was Nick's. Justin wanted to see him more than anyone, but not now. Go away. Disappear again.

"Get in the car!" Nick shouted.

Justin glanced at him but didn't stop walking. At the end of the block, an old tree root broke through the sidewalk. When he got to it, he'd jump over it like he'd done on every walk home before Nick started driving him places.

"Get in the car." Nick's engine revved and the car heaved forward and stopped again next to him as he walked.

Behind him, Matt and his friends laughed. "Get in the car. Come sit on my stick shift."

Justin cringed, but Nick ignored them. The engine noise blotted out reality; Justin almost put his hands over his ears. When Nick got out of the car and appeared at his side, his hand going around his arm, Justin's eyes went to the boys. He wished they hadn't. They didn't deserve his eyes. He didn't want to care what their reactions were to Nick touching him, but he pulled his arm out of Nick's grasp.

"Is that them?" Nick said. "Is that them?"

"Leave me alone," Justin said.

Ahead, the tree root humped out of the ground. It was bigger than he remembered. Maybe the tree was getting ready to fall over. Maybe the tree wanted to save him and crush the boys under it.

"Where the fuck are you going?" Nick said.

To the tree root. When he reached it, he jumped over it.

"Are you them?" Nick said.

Justin stood by the tree to watch. Matt had transformed into a different person, fearful instead of cocky, careful instead of mean. But he had his friends with him. They were relaxed with their hands in their pockets. Their bad skin shone, and the sun wet their gelled hair.

"Them who?" Matt said.

"You know," Nick said. "You know what I'm referring to."

"We weren't doing anything," Matt said. "We weren't bothering you, right, Justin?"

"No," Justin said. He detached from the tree and crossed the street. If Nick thought he could disappear and not say anything about it, he was wrong. From across the street, Justin turned to watch Nick and the boys. He walked backward, unable to take his eyes off them.

"You know what I'm referring to," Nick said again.

Justin froze on the corner of Laurel Road, a small street with only four houses on it. Soon he'd be home, locked in his room. Nick would not come there. Keep walking. They won't bother you anymore. Now they would be totally disgusted by him because they'd know what he and Nick had been doing, and maybe they wouldn't want to come near him again. Or maybe Nick had made things worse. Two girls on bikes zipped by and briefly swiveled their heads, but didn't stop.

At the corner, he turned around. A scene from a cartoon. The sky above bright neon blue against the red and yellow leaves. Nick struck Matt on the crown of his head with his fist. Matt's eyes and mouth popped open. The force of the blow connected Justin to the other boys. The same horror on his face appeared on their faces. Matt folded at the knees, and Nick gripped him by the shoulders and brought him down. He beat the boy's head into the sidewalk while Sean and Kyle ripped at his clothes, trying to stop him. With each strike against the pavement, Justin flinched. He wanted to run and stop Nick, but his legs wouldn't move. He would run away and never speak to Nick again. Pretend he never met him. Nick jerked awake, as if out of a trance, wrestled himself away from the boys, and jumped into his car. The boys attacked the car, and as he peeled away, they were repelled from it. Sean fell to the ground next to Matt, and Kyle ran yelling out of sight.

Justin walked fast in the other direction, along Laurel Road. He didn't run, afraid someone in one of the houses was watching him. At the end of Laurel Road, he started running until he didn't recognize the houses. He heard his own crying and heaving. He coughed and sucked air into his lungs. He wouldn't stop running even when vomit spilled out of him.

The day Justin's apartment building in Albany collapsed, he got off the bus after work and saw rubble. He thought it was the building next door. Police cruisers and fire engines blocked a lane of traffic. Someone cried somewhere. One of his neighbors paced nearby, a cigarette between her fingers, her face naked and ugly. She didn't cover it with her hands. Dust and smoke powdered the air. Some of it stuck to her wet cheeks.

Half the building remained standing. There, on the third floor, his apartment. The wall on the left side of the building had collapsed, exposing the three apartments, like someone had peeled a lid off a can. In another room, a dress flapped on a hanger, the linoleum floors bent downward, as if melting. His possessions exposed. It took him a minute to recognize them. All of the cabinets in the ruined kitchen were open. He wanted to fly up the stairs to save his books, but the police wouldn't let him go. The building was unstable. He carried his bag with him, inside which were two extra shirts, a book, and little else. He didn't care about the furniture. Most of it he had acquired free from the side of the road. But the books; it killed him to leave them.

The police pushed the onlookers back behind a barricade. The base of the building was littered with piles of bricks. A broken chair lay on the sidewalk. The gleaming porcelain of a toilet peeked out of the rubble in the alley next to the building.

Among the onlookers, Nick appeared, his phone in front of his face. He was taking photos or video of the scene, pointing his phone at the ruined building. Justin stared at him, disbelieving. Nick must be involved somehow. He sensed Justin there and turned the camera on him. Justin charged at him and grabbed the phone, but Nick held on to it and backed away. The crowd split to let them play this out, and Justin quit trying to get the phone.

"What are you doing here?" he said. Nick, whose body swelled against his clothes, who was stronger, slipped behind a small group of onlookers and hurried away. Justin ran after him, and the world smeared. Only Nick glowed clear and harsh.

Justin caught Nick again, this time reaching around him and grabbing him by his ridiculous beard. Nick screamed, and his wet eyes blobbed in front of Justin's face.

"Help," Nick shouted. "Help me!"

"You did this," Justin said.

Nick hit him in the mouth. Justin imagined his teeth plunging through the soft clay of his lips. His hands went to them and tried to hold them together, the pain rubbery and wet. From behind him someone shouted. "Greg!" The person appeared, a skinny man with thinning hair. "Fuck," he said, gaping with disgust at Justin, at the blood he tried to hold in his hands. "Greg, just let it go. Get out of here."

"He attacked me for no reason," Nick said.

Of course, Nick would have another name.

"Admit who you are," Justin said, surprised by his own calm.

A star of blood appeared on the sidewalk at his feet. Justin sat in front of it. The two men walked away from him, in the direction of the police and the crowd. Justin stood and crossed the street, a car nearly plowing into him. In the park, he pretended he'd gone for one of his daily walks. In the dripping public restroom, he wet paper towels until they became a cool mush, which he held against his bleeding lips. Either Nick had become another person, or he was dead, or he was still Nick and was pretending not to be, or he was long gone, somewhere Justin would never know.

Justin got through the door to Willa's apartment and fell onto the futon. He felt more at ease with Mrs. Flores than here in his own sister's home. He'd already lied and embarrassed Willa. He didn't know why. "I need to stay here," he said. "I need you."

Willa froze by the kitchen table. "I don't have it in me to care for sick people and care for you."

"Jesus, Willa."

"What do you expect?" she said. "The way you've been acting."

"You don't have a choice," he said. He examined her tired face. "I have nowhere else to go and I have nothing. I was trying to be okay, but I'm desperate. I'm desperate."

"We'll talk to Mom."

"She doesn't want me."

Willa had never been a cold person, but she didn't easily open up her life; she must have feared he would steal something from her if she allowed him to be a part of her life for any longer, if they were to be brother and sister, friends. He'd settle for being her neighbor if she'd allow it. She didn't want him there unless she'd placed him herself, with tweezers. He didn't want to interrupt her plans, whatever they were. All he needed was help. Only a little.

"I'm not bad luck," he said.

"I'll give you money."

"You want me to go away so badly," he said, and laughed. A nervous hiccup sound that embarrassed him immediately.

He lay back and brought his balled hands to his face. Willa came around the coffee table and knelt on the floor in front of him and took his hands. She held them and tried to pry his fingers out and straighten them, but his hands wouldn't let her unclasp them. Soon, he wouldn't be able to move at all, and breathing would be a struggle. He closed his eyes. She tried harder, dug her fingers under his, pulled at his hands to try to get them away from his face. He didn't want to see her face, didn't want to know by looking at her how much she hated him. He almost laughed at her exertions, though it hurt him.

• •

Willa sat at the kitchen table with untouched tea in front of her, her phone in her hand. She wanted to call Luke, but what would he do to help? Justin's breath rattled from the futon. At one point, she rose from the table to check on him, bent with her face in his face, and watched a thin stream of drool run from his open mouth. He was sleeping.

She called her mother and let the phone ring and ring until the machine answered. She hung up and called again. When Grace answered, Willa had forgotten how she'd planned to start the conversation.

"Are you crying?" asked her mother.

"I don't know what to do. I need you to help me. Can you come here?"

"Is it your brother? Why didn't you tell me he was here? He showed up at my door looking like a drug addict. I wish I'd had some warning."

"Please come."

"What's wrong with him?"

"I think he needs a psychiatric evaluation," Willa said. "I could use your help. If you'd come here and try."

"I'm no help to him," her mother said. "He won't listen to me. He just stormed out when I tried to talk to him."

On the futon, Justin stirred and stretched. He sat up. His eyes glowed at her. They were white against his dark hair and beard, which had grown in more over the last few days.

"Okay, Mom," Willa said. "Never mind."

"Tell her to stay away," Justin said. He rose from the chair and stood in front of her. His eyes wild and large. She had not been afraid of him until now. On the other end of the line, the phone clicked and the call ended.

"She wouldn't come anyway," Willa said.

He walked to the counter and opened the drawer next to the sink and removed her kitchen knife. Willa scraped the chair against the floor as she stood. He held the knife out at her. Her face twitched.

"Are you going to stab me?" she asked, and they both laughed at the idea. Of course, he would never hurt her. Still, her heart leapt with her laughter.

"I just got this feeling like I wanted to be rearranged,"

he said. "Like all of my molecules could come apart and fly back together."

The tension between them dissolved. He brought the knife up and dragged it along his neck, dropping it before reaching his throat. She thought he'd mimed it, until the blood, after a slight delay, emptied onto the skin of his neck and darkened his shirt. A pump of it. Foam racing to the top of a beer bottle. He looked surprised that he'd done this to himself. Had it been a whim? As if he was trying death out. Maybe he hadn't expected the knife to be so new and sharp.

She pulled a tea towel from the counter and pressed it hard against the wound. Together they dropped to the floor. She grabbed his hands and made him hold the towel while she reached for her phone on the table. He gagged, and his head nodded around on his spine. Obviously, he didn't have the stomach for what he'd done.

In the ambulance, his eyes were glassy and woozy. She didn't see blame in them, but she'd failed him; she'd chosen to fail him. Someone else—another sister, someone resourceful and heroic—could have saved him.

Justin ran all the way from Laurel Road. When he got to Nick's, he hoped Nick would be there, and that he'd hallucinated what happened after leaving school. It would mean he was crazy, but it would be better than reality. Nick slamming Matt's head into the sidewalk. He saw it in his mind, replayed on a loop.

At Nick's, Justin tried all the windows until he found an open one, and with some trouble, he slid inside Nick's apartment, into the bathroom, and rested for a bit on the mossy rug in front of the bathtub. No sounds in the rest of the apartment except for the heat ticking on and the hot water running through the pipes. Justin removed his jacket and his soiled shirt, which he rolled up and threw in the trash.

Nick might not come back. He might go away and save himself. Did the boys know him? Maybe. He'd only been out of school a couple of years, not long enough for people to forget. Really, Justin didn't know much about Nick. Only what he liked during sex, and the kinds of video games and movies he enjoyed. Where were his parents? Why hadn't he gone to college? He rented this apartment and did whatever he wanted. He worked at a gym, and he'd been able, somehow, to move into his own apartment right after school.

At the exercise machine in the living room, Justin selected much less weight than Nick could lift and did a few reps until sweat sheened his skin.

The phone on the computer desk rang. Nick was the only person in his life who had a cell phone. Someday, he'd have enough money to get one for himself. Nick must have run out quickly to have forgotten it. It screamed on the desk and Justin unfolded it and put up the antenna.

"Nicky? Hello?" said a man.

"Yeah," Justin said.

"I've been calling you. Can I see you?"

"I don't know, can you?" Justin said.

The man paused. "Is this Nick?"

"You might have to wait a little to see me," Justin said. "Maybe forever." The phone almost slid out of his wet hand. He saw himself in the window across the living room, his white body like a ghost trapped in the glass.

"Who the fuck is this?" the man said.

Justin closed the phone and put it on the desk.

• •

Willa answered the door and found the police standing there. Two officers. They were looking for Justin, they said. We're looking for Justin Dunham. "Yes, he lives here," she said, and a twist occurred at the front of her brain, as if she'd done something wrong. Given him away. Stupid. They already knew he lived here.

In a panic, she obeyed them. But he was not in his bedroom when she opened the door. She hadn't seen him after school. She and Grace had been watching TV when the knock came. She'd been holding her US history textbook in her lap and felt the heaviness on the skin of her thighs.

The two officers stood in the kitchen. Did they know her father? They sat at the table with Grace.

Did they know where he might be? the officers asked.

No, they didn't.

It occurred to Willa to tell them she'd seen a man in a car parked outside the school, waiting for Justin, but she decided not to. Not when they'd explained that Justin had been involved in an assault. The victim in serious condition.

"Assault?" her mother said.

Willa shrugged, a stupid thing to do, as if her mother had asked her if Justin had eaten the rest of the potato chips. Grace wouldn't cry in front of the officers.

"We don't know the extent of his involvement," one of the officers said. "But the other victims we interviewed said he knew the perpetrator."

Grace turned to Willa. "What have you seen? What has he been doing?"

"I don't know," Willa said.

"Are there any friends you can tell us about?" one officer said. He spoke quietly to Willa, as if trying to make Grace and his partner disappear. "It's the friend we're interested in. All we need is information from your brother."

"He has no friends," Grace said. She turned her wedding ring over and over, then stopped and put one hand on the other.

Willa looked at the front door, expecting him to come home and see her betray him. "I saw a man in a car," she said. "Who picked him up after school."

"What kind of car, if you remember?"

"A man?" her mother said. "Excuse me?"

"I don't know anything," Willa said. "I don't know."

· ·

He was alone in the apartment for ten minutes, still sitting at the weight machine, when Nick surprised him. He appeared from behind, not from the front door. "You're here?" Nick said. His eyes were dry. He raced around the room and glanced out the windows.

"What do you want me to do?" Justin said. "Where should I go?"

"Fuck. Fuck. Fuck. We're in big trouble," Nick said.

"I came here," Justin said. "And you weren't here."

"I've been driving around looking for you. I've been driving around thinking any second—"

"You were? You have to run away."

"Yes," Nick said. "We need to go now." He found a duffel bag in the hall closet and put things into it.

"You hurt Matt," Justin said.

"I had to. He shouldn't have touched you, and then he

was a smart-ass with me. What did he expect?" Nick pulled clothes out of drawers. He threw a shirt at Justin.

"Are you really here?" Justin said.

"Did you bring anything? Any clothes?"

"No. I didn't go home."

"We'll buy some for you. Quit sitting there!"

Justin abandoned the weight machine and put on the shirt. "What should I do?"

If he called Willa, what would he say if she answered? She'd want to help, even if they weren't friends anymore. It was his fault they weren't; he'd been ignoring her, but she wouldn't care about that, not if he was in trouble.

"Do you think the police will want to talk to me?" he said. "I didn't do anything."

"What the fuck do you think?"

"But I didn't do anything."

"It's your fault this happened," Nick said. "You're the whole reason. I'm not going to be the only one who gets in trouble."

"I want to go home. I didn't do anything." Justin picked up his jacket and backpack and slipped both on.

"Stop saying that!" Nick grabbed him by the arm and they left the living room and climbed out a window in the bedroom. They walked through the gravel lot behind the apartment house and into the grass. Once under the cover of trees, Nick let his arm go.

"You're involved, because we're together. If the person you're with hurts somebody, and you know about it, and you don't do anything to stop them, it's like you did it. But why would you want to abandon me anyway? What kind of person are you?"

"I'm sorry," Justin said.

They reached the car, and it frightened him in the dark. Somehow, it had been left in the woods, as if it had sat for years with bushes and weeds growing around. It didn't belong here under the canopy. Moonlight barely touched it through the trees.

"Is that your car?" Justin said.

He opened the door and yes, it was Nick's car. There was the crack in the dashboard with the duct tape peeling off, the CDs of bands Justin had never heard of.

When they started moving, he opened the window to hear the sound of twigs and small plants crackling under the tires. Nick drove out slowly, along a hiking path not made for cars. They'd only driven for a few minutes, but he was already motion sick. He gripped the seat, hoping they wouldn't get stuck in mud. The path was wide and cleared of debris, but now and then a fallen branch would scrape the side of the car.

The woods spit them into a field and Nick brought the car onto the road. The bump from the field to the road put him over the edge.

"I'm going to puke!"

"I can't stop," Nick said. "Stick your head out the window."

He did, and painted the side of the car with bile.

"Is this how you're going to be?" Nick said.

Justin settled back in the seat and buckled his seat belt. Nick looked into the rearview again and again, and seemed to be watching his speed, taking it slow until they reached the thruway. The roads were peaceful in a strange way, as if everyone was hiding from them. Maybe this was a dream. Just a quiet dream about driving around with his boyfriend.

Something had lodged in Justin's throat, large enough that he couldn't breathe around it, and now it sank into his stomach, which inflated and became hard. He put his hands on it and rubbed to comfort himself.

• •

Justin started feeling better and freer when the sun disappeared completely. No lights lined the highway. He didn't have to go home. They were going to end up somewhere and live there together. They would be fine. Nick played with the radio, giving up on it when he couldn't find anything good.

"Where are we going?" said Justin.

Nick kept quiet. Maybe he was too upset to speak. Once in a while, headlights appeared behind them and illuminated the car, grew closer, and flew by. Each time, Justin's muscles tightened and unclenched. They had been driving for an hour.

"No one's following us," Justin said.

"I have a friend in California. Jimmy Delgado."

"Oh," Justin said.

"Yeah. He lives somewhere close to L.A."

"Does he know we're coming?"

"We're not. I don't know what we're doing yet. I didn't have time to plan, you know?"

"I'm sorry," Justin said.

"Stop saying you're sorry. You said it five hundred times already."

Far ahead, a deer galloped across the road and Nick eased off the gas. In the field to their right, a herd of them stood, all waiting for the car to pass. In the side-view, he barely made out the shapes of their bodies moving into the road.

"Is it okay if we pull over?" Justin said.

"Why?"

"Just for a minute."

Nick brought the car to the shoulder and put it in park.

"Turn off the car," Justin said.

"You want to piss in the dark, go ahead."

Nick turned off the engine. In the blackness, the stars intensified. The windshield was like a screen of them. Justin undid his seat belt. He loved the feeling of sitting in the dark with the car cooling and ticking, as if they were inside a warm, strong animal.

Justin climbed onto Nick's lap and straddled him, squeezing between Nick and the steering wheel.

"What are you doing? Get off me," Nick said.

Justin kissed him. He rarely initiated kissing. He didn't want to hear Nick's anger. He blocked it with his tongue. Nick's hands ran over his back.

"Thank you," Justin said. "Thank you for protecting me."

That Justin might want to escape his life didn't surprise Grace. She put the phone on the table. The kids downstairs pounded from one end of the apartment to the other, the TV blared. Always fighting. She went into the bathroom to confront herself and get ready. Justin needed her, Willa said. But that was something you said to people. Did he really need her? What would she do for him? He'd tried to kill himself somehow. It didn't matter how. It was that he'd done it.

See? Willa said. *See?* Grace took that to mean *See what you've done to him?* But what had she done? They were in each other's lives so little now. She'd felt a similar uselessness when he'd run away at seventeen, when he'd been hurt. She'd stood in the hospital room watching him. Not sleeping. Not awake. She hadn't been able to stop him, to prevent it, and she couldn't help him. What kind of parent were you if your children wouldn't follow you?

When he was a baby, she'd suspected trouble. He cried in terror when his father held him. He wanted Grace, only Grace, all the time. He was her first, and she loved him and did what you were supposed to do. Gave away her sleep and her body. Some months into his life, his body stopped working. He became a little drum filled with gas and waste. He howled like a fox. She and Arthur spent hours walking around the house with him, driving him in the car. She cried with him and hated him. Little screwup! If he would only let her eat and sleep and shower.

He never did warm to his father. Arthur tried. She placed sleeping Justin onto his father's growing beer belly, onto the bare skin, so that it would bond them. He resisted school too. One day, and she'd never forgotten this, Arthur had lugged him over his shoulder, out of the house, and put him on the bus. Justin had cried and cried because he didn't want to go. The driver asked Arthur to take him off the bus. He was six years old. Back in the house, he collapsed on the couch and wailed. He became a problem for the teacher, who barely held back her disdain for him. Grace met with her and sensed rottenness inside the other woman as they discussed Justin, but Grace also understood the frustration. Why couldn't he stop crying, adjust to school, make their lives easier?

In the bathroom, she brushed her teeth and combed her hair. She couldn't afford to dye it anymore. The price kept rising, and with her bad shoulders, she was unable to do it herself. Willa promised to help, but never found the time. She worked long hours and when she visited, she wanted to relax, not fuss with hair dye. Her hair hadn't turned that fashionable silver. It had gone iron-colored.

If Arthur were here, he would guide her. They would be in the car already, on the way to the hospital. If Arthur had lived, maybe things would have been a little different for her. Not for Justin, really. He would have done whatever he wanted; it was how he was born, something in his blood. He would still be Justin. He would still have gotten involved with that *person*. But maybe she wouldn't have had to suffer him. Arthur would have taken some of it. Arthur would have helped her do what you were supposed to do. Run to places when your child was hurt. Here she was sitting on the couch, here was the remote in her hand and the news going.

Part Two

THE WOODS

M rs. Flores," he said like someone in an old movie, when she opened the door. Mrs. Flores, as if he were saying *good day*. Perhaps she'd let him in and have him *do* something, instead of just sit and watch her TV. It was all he did up in Willa's apartment. And then he came down to Mrs. Flores's apartment and did the same thing.

She watched morning news shows, and fluff shows, where they demonstrated how to make easy meals for one, or simple crafts. Justin followed her into the living room and flipped to a movie channel and settled on whatever appeared. Together they watched murder scenes, sex scenes, and gun fights. He stared, unmoved by all of it.

"I told you to call me René," she said.

"I can't."

"Why not?"

He didn't answer.

"I could use your help with something," she said, and pointed to a pile of her husband's golf magazines that she'd been keeping for no reason. His fingerprints were on the pages, that was all. It meant nothing to have fingerprints. They were invisible.

She handed Justin twine and asked him to tie the stack, as well as the newspapers and other periodicals she'd never gotten around to reading, and he lugged them to the curb. When he came back, she had him stand on a chair and brush off the dust strands and cobwebs where the ceiling met the wall. He really was a tall person. He kept the healed wound on his neck covered.

"Can I stay for a little longer? Vacuum or something?" He reminded her so much of the little boys who used to live in the neighborhood and would come around during the winter and ask to clear the driveway.

"If you do all the cleaning," she said. "I'll have none to do myself and I'll sit in a chair and die."

René had always cared too much about what went on in other people's houses and minds. For years after her retirement, she went through a period of adjustment during which she couldn't stop gazing out the window at all the wrong occurring on this street with frustration and helplessness. She'd been a social worker, walking into neighborhoods not far from here, knocking on doors and invading the lives of people who did not want to see her, who feared she would be instrumental in taking their children away.

Justin had asked to stay with her, and though she'd offered him a place here weeks ago, she'd had plenty of time to think about it. Of course, it had flown out of her mouth when she talked to her daughter Brianna on the phone, and Brianna made her promise she would not let Justin into the house again. A grown man, not a child. A grown man who had wielded a knife and cut his own throat. But no, René explained, Justin wasn't dangerous. Still, she'd promised Brianna he wouldn't stay.

She couldn't help him. And he did nothing for her except make noise in another room when otherwise there would have been silence. Without them discussing it, he would fall asleep on the couch and she would cover him with a blanket.

• •

René's heart was failing. Brianna visited most evenings after work, and René made sure Justin was gone by then. After Brianna left, she was alone. Night terrified her. René piled pillows behind her head, because when she lay flat, fluid gurgled into her throat and she awoke with the sensation that she was drowning, and her heart pounded, and she focused too much on its beating. This kept her awake for a long time.

In the dark, she heard Justin upstairs. Also awake.

"I don't sleep anymore," he'd told her. "I think I'm so tired that I want to sleep too much, and you can't have the thing you want too much."

"When you fall asleep on my couch, you are adequately asleep."

She didn't try to sleep tonight. In the musty chair in the living room, she put the TV on, the volume low so she wouldn't bother Willa, who worked so hard. The people in the TV screen busied themselves, disappeared and morphed into new people. Around midnight, there was a knock on the door.

"I had to listen really hard, but I heard your TV," Justin said.

"Take off those boots if you're going to put your feet on my couch," she said.

He bent to untie his boots and left them by the door. She found his youth attractive, but he wasn't handsome. She liked more clean-cut types. Brianna's father had been breathtaking when she met him, and as he aged, he developed a new kind of beauty. He grew a mustache and kept his hair neatly parted to the right. His skin darkened slightly, so he resembled photographs of his father in Mexico in the 1930s.

Justin didn't stay up chatting. He climbed onto the couch fully clothed and slept with one of her fleece blankets wrapped around himself. During a commercial, she watched him. What a development, this man on her couch. Dressed like a big teenager in black jeans. She didn't have a son, and didn't want Justin to be hers, but if he were her son, she'd be worried, possibly ashamed that he had ended up on her couch. At a respectable hour, she went into the yard to check on the flowers. She'd forgotten to water. There'd been no rain for weeks, and with Justin in her hair, she'd forgotten. But that was cruel. He wasn't in her hair. He occupied space in her mind, which wasn't a terrible thing. Oh, it wasn't his fault the flowers died.

Just as she was thinking of him, he appeared from behind her. He moved carefully, not yet fully awake.

"I should have said something." He crouched to inspect the violas and pansies. "I kept walking by them and I was afraid to say something. I thought maybe you *wanted* to kill them."

"Why would anyone want that?"

He pulled them out and tossed the yellowed and twisted corpses onto the grass. René had never been any good at growing things, but she kept trying it, either flooding her plants to death or forgetting them altogether. Some things you never get any better at.

One night in mid-October, Justin went to René's after walking home from his group meeting. The smell of pumpkins drifted through the air from a nearby farm. There were five people in his group, not including the therapist, Jake, who had a tattoo of a dragonfly on his cheek.

"A tattoo on his face?" René said.

"I've never seen one, either," Justin said. He'd brought her takeout from the Thai place on Main Street. She ate only a little. He realized too late that the food would be too salty.

"I don't need the group," he told her. "I feel well enough to never go again. I want to work more. Three days isn't enough."

A temp agency had placed him in an office on the nearby college campus. The other clerks, all women, had worked there forever, and he was new and young to them. They commented on his youth often, but he didn't feel young. They handed him files, which he piled onto his desk until there were enough to keep him busy at the wall of cabinets. No one asked him about the scar on his neck.

"It's not my business, but that's a terrible idea," René said. "Give yourself some time. Stay in group."

"I need to make money and get away from Willa."

"Don't say that. She's important for your happiness."

"How can I get better when she's my witness?"

"That's not her fault, either," René said. "You hurt yourself in front of her because you wanted to hurt her. You didn't really want to hurt yourself."

"I guess," he said.

After dinner, while she scraped food into Tupperware, he went into the bathroom to splash water on his face. The feeling of a knife opening skin. What had it felt like and what had it looked like? For the past few weeks he'd tried to access the memory, confront it. Willa didn't talk about it. One drop of blood couldn't be removed. It had jumped from him and onto the carpet. You have to tear the whole carpet up if the stain won't come out. When he told René about it, she said, "That's a good carpet."

In the hall, he passed René's bedroom, with the purple light coming through the window. What a disaster! Clothes and papers and things scattered. The jewelry box on her dresser, opened and vomiting necklaces. She'd been searching for something. She had hardly eaten. When he came in earlier, he'd found her sitting in her chair in front of the TV. *You've been there all day*, he wanted to scold her. *Imagine, the King of Sloth.*

"What's going on?" he said, confronting her in the kitchen, her back to him. She finished rinsing out the takeout containers and put them in the recycling bag under the sink.

• •

"Maybe you should leave René alone," Willa said. They were in the kitchen cleaning up after dinner. Justin had made pancakes, the only thing he knew how to cook. Willa and René were both trying to teach him more. In Albany, he'd gotten used to takeout and sandwiches from the deli counter at work.

He'd been waiting for two months for Willa to say something to him about René. She'd let October and November go by, and he took her silence as approval of his friendship with René, of his decision to essentially live with her. Now he knew René was sick, that her heart was slowly failing, that Brianna would be around more and more because of this. He couldn't be a burden to her, too. He hated thinking of himself that way. Why couldn't he visit? Maybe help her somehow.

Willa didn't want to deal with a Christmas tree, so Justin had walked to the store and bought a string of lights to hang on the bookcase. They were large multicolored bulbs that reminded him of being a kid. He glanced at them from the kitchen as he washed the dishes. He tried to feel brightness. "I'm just going to check on her sometimes."

"Brianna doesn't want you around."

"René does."

"Justin."

"You can invite Luke over," he said. "We could have a Christmas party. I'll ask René and Brianna if they want to come."

After they finished cleaning, she disappeared into the bedroom. On the way down the stairs to René's apartment, he decided not to knock on the door to bother them. Brianna's car sat in front of the house at the curb. It gave him a crick in his heart. He'd seen less and less of René.

With Brianna around, he saw himself through her eyes. Pathetic, childish man, bothering her mother. An old woman who was too nice to complain. What did he want from her? He imagined Brianna saying it to René. *If he checks on you now and then, Mom, I'd get it. But he wants to see you every day. It's not normal.*

René had told him one morning, exhausted and altered from the lack of sleep, that she loved the idea of his sleeping body in her house, and he'd blushed because it had been such an intimate admission to make. As if she'd said she loved his nakedness.

He'd do little chores and sit with her, bring her things to eat, which she'd ignore. But it was good to be around someone who knew little about him. He could love that person easily.

Willa waited for Jenny. Her mother was finally asleep, the police gone. She had called Jenny to invite her to go looking for Justin. She knew they wouldn't find him, but Jenny would come anyway, and it was better than sitting in her room waiting for the sun to come up.

Where should she start? This is when you're tested about a person. What did they like to do? Where did they hang out and with whom? Did they want to be quiet and alone, to figure things out, or did they not think at all? Did they jump into something terrible, something that might kill them? Willa only knew old things about Justin. She didn't know if he had friends other than the man in the car. Even if she'd asked him about his life outside the house, he wouldn't tell her. It wasn't her fault she didn't know him.

Jenny arrived at the house and dropped her bike on the lawn, and they hurried around the side of the house and into the back field. They ran through a giant bubble of freezing air that had been trapped in the tall grass. It broke apart and shot through their clothes. Willa squealed.

"Why are we doing this?" Jenny said. She pulled out flashlights from her bag and tossed one to Willa. Always prepared. Willa hadn't thought about flashlights. "Justin is a jerk. You don't even like him."

She hadn't told Jenny about the police, about the "assault." Jenny hadn't heard it from anyone, yet. Willa told her Justin had not come home. She didn't want to sit and do nothing.

"I don't want him to be *gone*," Willa said. But he was gone. He wouldn't be in the woods, or anywhere. They were playing a stupid detective game. He'd vanished.

When they reached the little brook, Willa sat on the slab of shale she and Justin used to play at during their early summers, when they would sneak away. They weren't allowed to play in the woods alone but did anyway. There was something nice about being next to water, especially clear water. They liked to watch what the brook carried. One day, Willa found a man's driver's license. Justin said she had to try to get it back to him, but she wanted to keep it. By the time they got to the house, Justin had forgotten about it anyway, so she'd kept the license. It was somewhere in her room. Once, she'd seen the man in town and thought: *Newson, Garrett, 12/7/60.*

An animal moved nearby, and Jenny pulled something out of her pocket and there was a flicking noise. Willa turned the flashlight on her and revealed a switchblade. She laughed hard from her place on the rock. Jenny had loved *The Outsiders* when they read it in seventh grade.

"It's my dad's. It's not like I bought one for myself."

"What are you going to do with it?" Willa asked.

Jenny put the knife away. "I don't think he's in the woods. I don't think he's hiding in a tree."

• •

In town, they held on to their flashlights and lit the way with a concentrated spotlight on the sidewalk. No cars passed on Front Street. In the distance, the lights in the parking lot of the Village Green glowed, though the stores, restaurant, the park and pool were all closed. They walked along Locust Park's chain-link fence. Willa hadn't been on the other side of the fence for a long time. The last time, she'd been young enough to be swinging on the swings.

Voices echoed out of the park. When a group of boys came into view, she and Jenny turned off the flashlights. The boys huddled around a fire inside a grill by the picnic tables. One of the boys disengaged from the group and hopped onto a table and pissed off the end of it calmly. He wasn't making a statement, just pissing wherever he wanted. His pee splattered onto the ground and the end of the bench tucked under the table. Boys lived inside a different sphere of the world, next to her own. A free, repellent place.

"Let's turn around," Jenny said.

But Willa saw the boys were not laughing, not having a good time. They were talking, all through gritted teeth. Some crying. Four of them, including the pissing boy, who rejoined them. Justin would never be one of them. They were his enemies, and they were hurting now. One of the boys turned and noticed them. The fire illuminated his face and showed he hadn't been crying after all. He was angry, the kind of anger that lasts and lasts. If he spoke to them, he would take out his anger on them. Jenny turned and Willa followed her.

She would never show her face at school again. She'd be expected to go tomorrow, but now she would be known. No one bothered with her, usually. She and Jenny were called lesbians because of their clothes and friendship, but they had each other's support and it didn't hurt as much as it could have. It didn't hurt Willa, at least.

An ache opened inside her, and it wouldn't let her think of anything else. Things had changed for her. If she ever saw Justin again, she would kill him for doing this to her.

"Hey!" the boy called after them. "Hey, did you know Matt? You can come over if you want!"

"Just keep going," Willa said, and Jenny walked faster.

S omewhere in western New York it had started to snow, and Nick decided to pull over and take shelter in a motel. They had only been driving for four hours. Justin wanted to be farther away from home before they stopped, but the snow fell heavily, making it impossible to see the road. He had not eaten anything since lunch and being in the car had started to make him dizzy.

They lay on a hard bed. Nick suggested Justin keep all of his clothes on, including his jacket. They wouldn't stay in a nice place. In shitty places, no one cared who you were. Did anyone care that Justin had left? The police must have come for him. They had spoken to Grace, probably. Willa would care. He was missing, or a runaway, or a murderer.

Nick was comforting him, because earlier they had fought. After they'd escaped the car and were behind closed doors, something inside Justin untwisted. Now that they'd stopped somewhere, had checked in to this motel using the names Jimmy and Nathan, it was real to him. They were never going back. They might be caught. If Matt was dead— he couldn't think of it, but couldn't think of anything else.

He wept and hyperventilated. He felt like a spinning top someone had let loose on ice. It was his fault someone had died. He moaned and knocked into the furniture. "What if you killed him?" he asked Nick.

Nick stopped him by putting his arms around him and squeezing.

"Shut up! Shut up!"

At first, Nick attempted to comfort him, but the pressure increased until Justin's face burned, and his scalp prickled. His eyes would leap from his skull! He stared at the painting on the wall. A goose with its beak open, running after a little girl. Moss-green grass and slate sky. He was going to die staring at that painting. Nick let him go and Justin fell onto the bed, light-headed but no longer panicked. Nick locked himself in the bathroom for a few minutes.

He came out and lay on the bed with Justin, stroked Justin's face and kissed him, massaged the sore muscles of his stomach and chest. He told him to breathe in slowly and not to move too much.

"Pretend it never happened," Nick said.

"I can't," Justin said.

"You better try," Nick said. "It didn't happen."

Nick kissed his neck and his ear. He freed Justin's dick from his jeans and swallowed it, and Justin came quickly, covering his face with his hands, unable to control the convulsions. He lay there with his pants open, Nick's head resting on his thigh.

• •

The next day, the snow stopped. A few inches on the ground. It was wet snow that slid off the car in clumps. The sky clear of clouds and bright and cold. They got back into the car and drove for a while until Nick pulled over again, parking the car in a gravel lot.

"Come on," Nick said, and got out of the car.

They walked onto a forest trail. The trees, caked with snow, bent around them. The quiet path went on and on. Through the trees, an oval of ice sparkled, a pool of water. No one knows we're here. No one will find us. He did something he never did: jumped onto Nick. Though he surprised him, Nick caught him and carried him on his back for a while and Justin reached some low branches and batted snow off them.

Nick's cell phone rang, as it had been doing on and off since they'd left. Justin slid off his back. Nick took the phone out of his jacket but didn't answer.

"It's the gym," he said. "I'm supposed to be there right now." He laughed. "I don't have a job anymore, I guess."

Nick waited for it to stop ringing and threw it into the woods, where it shattered against a tree.

"Why'd you do that?" Justin said.

"I don't need it anymore," Nick said. "I don't want it."

"But you have to call your friend, don't you? He doesn't know we're coming."

"It doesn't matter, Justin."

Justin searched the ground for pieces of the phone. Nick put his cold hands over Justin's eyes.

"No one can get in touch with us," Nick said. "We can't get in touch with anyone."

Back in the car, Justin fell asleep. When he woke up again, they were in Pennsylvania. Sometime later, they entered Ohio. Justin had never been to either place. Not much to see. Nick exited the highway and stopped the car in the parking lot of a grocery store. It was late, and there were hardly any cars. He turned off the headlights and hurried to the trunk. When he reappeared, Justin saw him running to a car and crouching by the back. He got out of the car to see what he was doing.

"You're going to get caught," Justin said.

Justin didn't like breaking rules. He glanced at the entrance to the store to see if anyone was coming out. In the bright yellow light inside, one cashier leaned against a register reading a magazine.

With a screwdriver, Nick struggled to remove a license plate from a car.

"I don't know," Nick said. "You think I know how to do this? If the police are looking for us, they know my license plate."

The screwdriver clattered against the plate. Nick couldn't get it off. He quit briefly, squeezing the screwdriver. Justin thought he might stab himself in the leg with it.

"Fuck it," he said.

"Do you think they have other cops looking for us? Like cops from here?" Justin said. "Do you think Matt's dead?"

Nick gripped the screwdriver again and strained to turn

the screw. With a squeak it came loose and soon he held the rusted plate in his hand.

"Watch the door and tell me if you see anyone," Nick said.

• •

It wasn't until they reached their next stop, another one-story motel, long and empty, that Nick got out of the car and removed the license plates and replaced them with the stolen ones from the grocery store parking lot. Justin watched him carry their original plates to the side of the motel building and frisbee them into the trees.

Inside, Justin took a shower. There were no paper-wrapped soaps or sample bottles of shampoo. He shut the water off, still dirty. In the room, Nick waited for him on the bed, naked. He'd spread out their jackets and clothes on top of the blanket and had tossed the pillows onto the floor. The TV was on, playing a movie Justin had never seen. On the screen, a baseball team argued in a locker room. Justin held his underwear in his hand. At some point, they would need to buy more clothes.

Nick spit on his hand and massaged his dick. He wanted to fuck, but Justin had never enjoyed it, hadn't mastered it. He hoped one day he would, but it wouldn't be here and now. His mind was elsewhere, back home. He wanted to give in to being with Nick forever, being free of school, his mother, all but Nick's body and attention, but he was too afraid.

"If you get on top of me, it'll be easier. You can control it," Nick said.

Justin climbed onto the bed and kissed Nick's chest and lips.

"Come on," Nick said. "Get on top of me." He slapped Justin's thigh.

Justin straddled him.

"You're not even hard," Nick said.

"I'm sorry."

"Whatever. It's okay." He took Justin's hand, spit into it, and guided it to his dick. Justin gripped it and tried to ease it inside himself. Nick's fingers probed him and slid inside. After several minutes, Nick turned and shoved Justin off.

"Get on all fours," Nick said.

"I don't want to," Justin said. "Can we do something else?"

"Justin. Are you with me or not?"

Justin flipped over and onto his knees. The room had turned cold. Nick never forced Justin to have sex. He'd never gotten angry if Justin didn't want to do certain things, but since they'd left, his patience with Justin seemed to have run out. "Yeah, I'm with you," Justin said.

"Get over here," Nick said. He grabbed Justin by the arm and pulled him to the edge of the bed. He turned him around easily and shoved his head onto the mattress and tried to enter him. The pain seared as he resisted Nick, and he begged for it to stop. He couldn't loosen up. Nick kept trying. Finally, he lost his erection.

Justin saw Matt's head cracking against the sidewalk. Was it once or twice? Had he really seen it happen? In his memory, he heard it. A sick, meaty sound. Nick had done it. The person standing behind him now, who he had run away with, had done it. Outside, the traffic hissed, people talked. He was sure the people could hear them through the thin walls, Nick's rough voice and Justin's own whining and struggling.

"Let me go," Justin said. "Please. You're hurting me."

Nick removed his hand from the back of Justin's head and Justin turned around. His muscles ached. Nick's penis hung shriveled and sad between his legs. He grabbed his jacket and pulled on his sweatpants.

Justin searched for his underwear. "Why are you so mad?" he said. He was getting tired of Nick's moods, and his torso still hurt from when Nick had squeezed him. Underneath, his heart pumped with unpleasant force.

Nick wouldn't look at him. He left, and Justin went after him, but couldn't follow him naked into the night. Nick got in the car, started the engine, and drove away. Light snow blew off the top of the car. Justin closed the door and took his jeans off the bed and put them on without his underwear. He put on several shirts and zipped his jacket. He sat on the edge of the bed and waited. If Nick didn't come back in twenty minutes, Justin would decide what to do next.

• •

Two hours later, Justin walked through the parking lot. There were no cars. Music played on a radio at the end of the squat building, and a rabbit sat watching him from a patch of gravel in the corner of the lot. When Justin moved, it escaped into the tall grass. Away from the single streetlamp, the world became country dark. It took time for his eyes to adjust, and when they did, he had trouble seeing where he was going. No clouds above, so the stars were out and bright. They glowed in the asphalt, as if caught there. Or he was sleepwalking and dreaming it. He walked for a while before having to stop. He'd never exhausted himself before, and thought he'd caught something from the filthy motel room. The flu or some disease he'd never heard of. His legs abandoned him, and he sat in the weeds.

The light in the sky changed. He dragged himself to his feet and continued walking. The cold had seeped into his butt cheeks and thighs. The woods reminded him of home, but it was a trick. If he entered, he would get lost and end up eating grubs or neon-red berries, which would burn on the way down his throat. He'd never learned how to survive, though he spent a lot of time in the woods behind the house in Locust. That time was spent hiding or jerking off. He didn't know the name of this fern or this wildflower, which berries were safe to eat, except for the obvious ones. Willa liked to learn those things. She and Jenny went hiking all the time. Willa bought field guides with her own money.

"You're stepping on trout lilies," she'd tell him, instead of calling them "flowers."

Somewhere farther along the road, he collapsed again. The sky had gone from black to gray, so he must have been walking a long time. The last thing he'd eaten had been a chocolate cupcake from a vending machine. He didn't wake until a vibration sparkled from his heels and through his calves. His sneakers dragged on the cement and someone's hands pinched his underarms. He kicked and whoever was dragging him let him drop. A short fall, but pain shot up his asshole and lower back.

"Get in the fucking car," Nick said, the skin on his cheeks and forehead bright pink, cold morning sweat in his hair.

"What do I do with you?" Nick said.

Would Nick squeeze him again, this time until his self popped out of the top of his head and spilled over him? Justin imagined himself back at home, but too afraid to go into the house. He would stand outside in the road, in the cold rain, waiting for Willa to notice him. By then, she'd have given up on ever seeing him again. She would think the worst, assume after a few days that he was dead. She'd remember not to smile in public, especially at school. She'd see him from the front window and think he was a ghost.

• •

They drove through a beautiful place. There were naked hills and tall evergreens. They'd passed a sign for a state park. A hawk sat on a bare branch down the road and turned its head to face the car as they neared it. For miles and miles since they left the motel, Nick hadn't spoken, and Justin hadn't been able to relax. He kept trying to read Nick's face.

"Stop looking at me," Nick said.

"You left me," Justin said. "That's why I left the motel."

"You don't want to be with me," Nick said.

"I'm scared," Justin said. He wanted to ask why Nick had been cruel last night, why he lost his patience so quickly. He wanted to say *please be good to me*, but he couldn't ask for anything more from Nick.

"I know he died," Nick said. "I killed him. Do you see the trouble I'm in? Or is this an adventure to you?"

"No," Justin said. "I want to go home." Yesterday, he wouldn't have said it. Today, it was all he wanted. To be away from Nick.

"You're not going home," Nick said.

Justin stared at the road through the windshield.

"You ruined my life," Nick said.

Nick threw a beef jerky stick at him and it landed in his lap. Justin hadn't eaten anything for the whole day they'd been in the car. He didn't want to eat. He let the jerky stay where it had landed. After a few minutes, Nick took it back and opened it. Justin's stomach sucked itself inward. If he jumped out of the car now and survived, he'd run into the wilderness and be eaten by a mountain lion.

"Don't eat," Nick said. "Whatever."

"I won't," Justin said.

• •

Justin put the radio on and flipped through station after station of static and preaching until he found music. As they drove out of the park, the trees became less grand. What state were they in?

When he woke, they were driving through a town of old buildings, many with boarded windows. In the distance, there were trees and rolling hills, brown and rust-colored leaves. A storm hovered far away and shed blurry snow on another town. People stood around outside the buildings. No other cars passed. A giant dog, a gray-and-brown mutt, galloped up the middle of the street. It wouldn't get out of the way. Nick would run it over without hesitation.

But he didn't. He stopped the car and Justin held his breath when the dog jumped. Its nails scraped and crackled on the hood. Nick honked the horn and the dog leapt off. Its large, muscled body tensed when it hit the road again, the legs so long and skinny Justin thought they would break, and he flinched. It galloped away.

People on the sidewalk stopped, some leaning on buildings or sitting on the curb. All men, and not entertained.

Justin waited to see what Nick would do, watched Nick's hands shaking before he gripped the wheel again. Though Nick had told him they were driving to California, Justin suspected they were really running nowhere. Nick put down the window.

"One of you own that dog?" Nick asked two of the old men standing by the side of the road, both pale-skinned and windburned on their noses and cheeks.

One of the old men opened his mouth, exposing blackness inside. Justin wished for a woman to appear. There must be children packed into an unseen school somewhere.

He was missing tests. Failing. Disappointing teachers who thought he was smart. He would not graduate, would be one of these men, standing on the side of the road in the middle of the day. It might be the perfect life for him.

"Freaks," Nick said. He drove forward a few feet and the car died. They were out of gas.

"You didn't get gas?" Justin said. He regretted the exasperation in his voice. He stared at the gauge, the needle pointed a tick below E.

Nick punched him. Caught him on the side of the mouth. The pain decided something for Justin. It sizzled and blinded him. He got out of the car and kicked the door until he left a mark.

Nick slipped on the gravel but came around to stop him. The dog watched them from down the road. The sun died on its dark, mud-caked fur; its tail hung and waved gently from side to side.

Justin avoided Nick and ran at the men. He sat on the sidewalk by the men's feet. "I'm going to stay here," he said. "I'll get home somehow. Leave me alone." He licked the blood from his mouth and cried. He'd never been punched before.

"Get the fuck up. Are you kidding me?" Nick grabbed him by the jacket, almost tore it off him. They fell onto the road together.

"I don't want to be with you anymore," Justin said.

"Shut up," Nick whispered, his anger barely caged. Spit leaked from his mouth and onto his sweatshirt. "What are you trying to do? You're going to get us in trouble."

The dog ran to them, barking, and hopped around until one of the men whistled at it. Nick shook Justin. "I'm sorry," Justin said. He kept saying it so Nick would stop shaking him. Nick twisted his fingers into Justin's hair and Justin rose to avoid the pain, pulling at Nick's fingers. Nick dragged him to the car and leaned him against it. One of the men shuffled away from the sidewalk and walked to the car. Some of the others laughed.

"Come here," the man said to Justin.

"My brother's a retard," Nick said to the man. "He gets out of hand."

"Come away from the car," the man said. He had an accent Justin hadn't heard before. Justin didn't want to go near the man. He didn't want to be near Nick, either. Nowhere to go.

"He ain't a retard," the man said. "I know what he is."

"We just want to get out of here," Nick said. He sounded afraid.

Justin's legs and shoulders ached. He didn't want to talk to the man or listen to what Nick might say, so he got back into the car. With the door closed, he still heard Nick lying to the man.

"Our parents are dead. I'm not good at controlling him," Nick said.

Justin expected the dog to appear any minute. It would leap at Nick and tear out his throat. Justin would flee, riding the dog, his hands in its bloody fur.

In the secrecy of her workroom, Willa sculpted a miniature of the new Justin with polymer clay and baked him in the oven like a gingerbread man. She gave him black jeans and all. A little beard. Considered putting a knife in his hand. It took a lot of mixing to find the right color brown for the beard. She thought of the beard as black, but of course it wasn't. She placed the magnifier in front of her eyes and tickled the color onto the face of the small Justin figure with the thinnest brush she owned. He couldn't know she was doing this. If he did find out, she would tell the truth. It hadn't been a conscious choice, and she didn't have plans for him. She hadn't built a box or a stage for him. After a time, she laid him on the desk to dry.

All of the scenes she'd created over the years climbed the walls on all sides of her. She kept them, though nothing pleased her. They pissed her off or embarrassed her. The miniature evergreens made her happy; they were the first miniatures she ever owned. Bought or stolen, she didn't remember. They made her happy because she had nothing to do with their creation. She should hate them, as they'd caused an obsession, a desire to shrink the world and make it manageable. Why did she think she should create Justin? As if you could make something small and understand it better.

Later, she drove to Luke's without calling. She often forgot to call him or text him and check in. Now that Justin lived with her, Luke didn't come over the way he used to, and she'd been okay without him, but here she was driving there and parking the car, going to the door. When he answered, she realized she'd missed him or missed some part of him. "Tell me you don't want to see me anymore," Luke said, and she put her arms around him.

"I'm used to you now," she said. "I don't want you to go away."

"But you can go away all you want, I guess."

He hadn't said it, but he was in love with her. She sensed it the same way you sensed that someone hated you. She ran her hands over his neck and shoulders and allowed herself to admire the strength of them. She could love him too. He wouldn't mind if it took a while. He would help her.

I'm relieved to see you," René said. Justin helped her from the couch into the wheelchair. She could walk, but got winded quickly.

René called him on the phone and asked him to come over. Brianna had gone to run errands. He'd been spending so much time alone in Willa's apartment. He didn't have a hobby. Reading put him to sleep now. The office didn't need him for more than ten hours a week. The year was almost over. The year he had hurt himself. The further it retreated into the past, the more he pretended it never happened. He tried to make himself presentable. Keep his beard trimmed, put product in his hair.

René's face had grown thin and the skin of her neck shook when he moved her.

"I've been busy," Justin said. "Work."

"Glad to hear it. Where are you taking me?"

"I haven't thought about it."

"Maybe we shouldn't," she said.

He helped her on with her coat and placed a blanket over her legs. During the walk, her breath billowed out of her mouth and traveled over her shoulder.

He pushed René all the way into town without noticing. The cold revived him. They'd reached the high school. Was it the same high school? His hands on the handles of the wheelchair looked carved out of soap, and he realized he'd dropped his gloves somewhere. He searched the ground for them. Before he turned the wheelchair around to head for home, a car sped by, going many miles over the school zone limit, and a passenger screamed something out of the window as they flew past. It set him off running, pushing René in the chair, but it was the type of running you do in dreams. Hard to make any progress. At the end of the road, he noticed that the hulking root, the giant tree that had once been his marker, had been removed. Or maybe this was another street, and not where he'd seen a boy killed. Matt DeRosa. It worried him how confused he was, but the street sign told him they were on Gaffney Road, not the same place it had happened, but it looked almost exactly the same.

"Justin?"

"Yes."

"It's cold," René said.

"We're going home," he said.

"Why were you running?" She sounded frightened and out of breath, as if she'd been the one running. Why had he taken her out of her warm house and worried her so much?

"Don't tell Brianna," he said.

"Did you know those people in the car?"

"I don't think so," he said. "But maybe they knew me."

Back at the house, he unwrapped her and found her

frozen. It had been too cold for her. The air too hard to breathe, thin and icy.

"Turn up the heat," she told him, and he went into the hall to the thermostat.

"I'm sorry," he said.

"I can't get warm," she said. She sounded afraid.

He helped her walk into the bedroom. His own bones ached. She sat on the bed and he helped her get her legs onto it and put the covers over them. He lay next to her and held René's cold body wrapped in the blanket until it matched his warmth.

"Justin," René said. "You don't have to stay."

"I shouldn't have taken you out," he said.

Her breathing slowed and grew textured.

Later, he awoke to the bright rectangle of the open door and a shadow eclipsing it partially. Brianna stepped into the room and turned around almost at once. He had fallen asleep next to René, she wrapped in her blankets, he curled next to her above them. Should he stay there and pretend he hadn't seen Brianna? Her voice drifted in from the kitchen, and by the time he stepped out of the bedroom, Willa had arrived to take him home.

Nick stood next to the car with the man from the sidewalk, the man who'd said he knew what Justin was. The fact that other men could see him always frightened Justin. They knew he wasn't like them. Nick could fake it, and it made Justin hate him a little bit. He would have felt better with someone weaker, someone more like him. Nick was one of them, really, wasn't he?

Justin rubbed his face and his hand came away covered in bloody mucus. Mud caked the front of his sweatpants and gravel pricked his heels inside his shoes. He sat in the passenger seat and the mud dried slowly on him. He would stay dirty. It would take a long time for Nick to calm down and trust him again, a long time before Nick would do anything nice for him.

Outside the car, one of the men poured gasoline from a can into the tank. "Now leave," the man said.

Nick got back in the car. His face was blank.

In the rearview, Justin saw the man with the gas can watching them go. He grew small quickly.

"Where are we going?" Justin said. The not knowing drove him insane. *Take me somewhere real*, he wanted to say.

Let's go somewhere we can stop and stay for a while. The car had become tight as a coffin. His head spun.

The tree-lined road went on for miles and miles without change. Any minute, the trees would break open and there would be a turn, a sign, a house. Something. But nothing appeared. He kept waiting. They must have skipped into a time loop. The trees disappeared and fields took their place, and when the fields ended, the trees reappeared. A dead raccoon on the side of the road was a relief. It meant another car had come by sometime in the past, and other cars might pass by again.

"You aren't on my side anymore," Nick said.

"Drop me off somewhere," Justin said. "I'll go home, and I won't say a word about you. I'll say I was afraid, so I ran away."

A sign for a numbered route appeared. Nick pulled over and kept the car running. Something had gone wrong with the car again. But no, Nick came around to the passenger side and opened the door. He waited at first, then bent and unclicked Justin's seat belt.

"Get out."

He's going to put me in the trunk. Or leave me. Justin slid out of the seat and tried to leap to the driver's side, but Nick grabbed him by the back of the neck and pulled him out of the car. He pushed him forward, forcing him to walk into the trees.

"Don't leave me here," Justin said. "Please don't leave me here." He'd run back to the town if necessary, even if the men there wouldn't help him. It would be better than going forward, walking on the endless road as the sun melted and the cold arrived. The pressure on the back of his neck increased. Nick's hand squeezed and a fan of pain spread through Justin's skull. His neck might break. It might break. He screamed, and the scream scattered into the trees. This was the biggest, most beautiful place he'd ever been. So big his scream struggled its way through the branches. The sun hid behind the trees as it set.

"Shut up," Nick said. Justin stopped screaming. Something had died nearby and rotted under the needles and leaves. Green ferns stuck out of the ground, though they curled and browned as if someone had come by with matches and burned their edges. Nick released him, and now that he was free, his head felt like it might flop off his body. Justin turned around to face him and almost tripped over a root. The ancient tree it belonged to towered behind him and he fell against it to steady himself and prepare to run. Nick's eyes showed no anger or sadness. He seemed tired, fed up. Justin could no longer find any love there.

"I'm sorry," Justin said.

"You're dangerous," Nick said. Justin didn't see what was in his hand until his arm went up. A long black object. It came down fast and struck him on the side of the head and made a ringing noise that ran away from them. Justin followed it. He ran toward the ringing and the ringing turned into Willa. He chased her to the creek in the woods behind their house, where they sat and put their hands in the water to wait for something good enough to grab to float by. But he hadn't gone anywhere. Nick's shoes crunched the ground by his face, and he breathed and breathed; the breath shaking out of him. Was Nick afraid of what he was doing? He didn't speak, didn't explain.

Once, a transformer blew close to the house in Locust. They'd all heard it. *Boom*, and the power had gone out. Willa had squealed. He remembered the sound of the "yipe" clearly in his right ear now. It was like Willa was here in the woods, making that frightened noise. Willa and their mother had lit candles all over the house and he'd wished they could live with lit candles forever.

He lay on the cold ground, smelling rotting leaves and crushed moss. Nick held the object up again and it clanged against Justin's head. He stared at Nick's eyes, which shone with tears that didn't spill. He fell on top of Justin, and Justin wiggled and tried to slide away, and tried to hit but wasn't strong, he'd never felt so weak. Nick had been right all along: the world would eat him alive. He hit Justin again, beating his chest and arms.

Justin passed out, woke, his own voice in his ears grunting. He flexed his muscles and went quiet. He promised himself he wouldn't breathe; he would pretend to die; he would die for real, anything to end the horrible feeling of Nick hitting him. With each hit, icy pain broke open in his head and body until he became numb. Out of the corner of his eye, a pool of black water appeared and said: *come here.*

B rianna closed René's bedroom door. Her hands and voice shook. She avoided Justin's eyes and being near him. Her hair was pulled tight and shiny. He briefly forgot he was a grown man, he felt so much like a little boy, the way she glared at him.

They stood in the hallway. "Is he a pervert, trying to seduce my mother or something?" Brianna asked Willa.

Willa laughed. "Are you fucking kidding me?" Justin wanted to embrace her. She held his arm. "First of all, my brother is gay."

"I walk in here," Brianna said. "And open this door and see him in bed with my mother. My mother who is sick and dying. Why are you here?" She almost screamed it into his face. From the bedroom, René's voice fluttered out. "Brianna, come here. Come here."

"I'm her friend," he said, but Brianna wasn't listening to him.

"I want him out of here," she said to Willa. "I don't care if he's mentally deficient or whatever he is. Get him out."

"I didn't do anything wrong," Justin said. "Your mother's my friend."

"We're leaving," Willa said. "Stop talking. This is ridiculous."

René would tell Brianna once she was calm. Nothing had happened. In his sleep, he'd found her and had taken her into his arms. Maybe it was stupid of him to do something like that, but he hadn't thought about it. She was cold and scared.

Willa's hand cuffed his wrist, and they left the apartment and climbed the stairs to her place. "Is it me or is she crazy?" Willa said. "Is she overreacting? You didn't do anything. She didn't see something you're not telling me?"

"Of course not," he said. "I would never hurt René."

"I know you wouldn't. Jesus. Justin, what were you doing?"

"Nothing."

What an imagination Willa must have when it came to him. To think he was capable of *anything*. Didn't she know what little power he possessed? She put a DVD of *Rosemary's Baby* on and talked to him over it, telling him she hoped he would not hold on to the bad feelings from what just happened. It would blow over. They both loved the movie and had seen it thousands of times. Justin had always liked the long, slow build of the plot, and the weird acting, Mia Farrow's deliberate way of talking, Ruth Gordon's terrifying wackiness. When she came on screen, they both shut up. Throughout the rest of the movie, he forgot and remembered what had just happened over and over again. He wanted to talk to René, to make sure she wasn't mad at him.

"I don't want Brianna to see you," Willa said, falling asleep. "It's better if she forgets about you completely."

Justin's bag sat on the floor at the end of the futon. Most of his stuff was inside it. His toothbrush, the new underwear, T-shirts. All his books were gone. The walls of his home were gone. All he had left were soft, useless things. He wouldn't make much noise as he left.

• •

In a bar, Justin was incapable of talking about the common interests of the other men, who all knew about the same things, who watched certain shows and movies and listened to certain music. They would sense his strangeness and avoid him. They would see he didn't know anything. He'd brought his clothes with him from Willa's; the stuffed bag sat at his feet. He ordered sodas and let the ice melt and dilute the carbonation until it turned into caramel water. As it grew later, the lights dimmed and heavier dance music switched on, though no one danced. The younger guys huddled together near the back of the place, all of them pretty drunk. A pair of older men played pool.

He didn't approach anyone, but after an hour or so a man sat next to him.

"I don't enjoy coming here," the man said. "But I force myself to."

Justin understood the man sensed this about him—he had forced himself to come in—and was trying to make a connection. He allowed it to happen. He smiled and ran his hand over his head. His hair was getting longer.

"I'm not a bar person, but what else are you supposed to do?" the man said. "I don't like the apps."

"I'm not, either," Justin said. "I'd like to leave. I've been here for a while."

The man was older, but not by much. Justin enjoyed his nervous energy. He felt powerful, and he rode the wave of the feeling. He didn't say much and avoided the man's eyes. He should look into someone's eyes, but it was difficult for him. He was out of practice.

"Don't leave yet," the man said, his face soft and slightly pocked. Not an intimidating face and not a bad face. Ten years ago, he'd probably been boyish. His hair reminded Justin of baby hair, soft and thin, and his scalp showed underneath.

"We could both leave," Justin said. He'd never been this confident, but the man put him at ease. Instead of walking, they would take the man's car, which was parked near the bar at the curb. He still heard the bass from the music. A few men stood out front smoking. At first, Justin hesitated, though this man wouldn't hurt him. He threw his things in the back seat and didn't pay attention to where they were going as they drove. He might as well have been blind-folded. He slipped out of the present and found himself in new places, with unfamiliar buildings all around. When they stopped, Justin reached into the back for his bag. If, for some reason, he would need to make it back to the bar, he'd be unable to do it.

The house they pulled in front of looked like so many

houses he'd seen around Willa's neighborhood. Old and boxy, but it was in good shape. The man had money.

Inside, Justin sat in a fancy leather chair. The man knelt on the floor in front of him and untied his sneakers.

"Where are you going?" the man said. "Are you traveling?"

The man owned beautiful things, though the house was small. Pictures of people from his life stood on the credenza and mantel. Loads of family and friends. Vacations to islands Justin would never see.

"Yes," Justin said. "I'm going out west." He wasn't.

"Out west?" the man said. He laughed a little. He removed Justin's sneakers and put them aside. "I saw you and thought you looked tired. You looked . . . you know, really good. But rough."

Justin's dick grew hard. He hadn't been with anyone for a long time. He had hardly touched himself. The man thought he was rough, but he'd never been. He tried to make his voice deeper when he answered, and he hated himself for doing it. Pretending, playing a game when he could have been himself. He'd never been able to hide his queerness. Hadn't been able to fake the kind of masculinity he didn't possess.

"Is that everything you own?" the man said.

"Yes," Justin said. The rest of what he owned had been destroyed. He wanted to warn the man. *I am someone who makes buildings fall. I am someone who makes people mad enough to beat me to death.*

The man peeled Justin's socks off and draped them over

the sneakers. His feet probably smelled by now. He'd been walking around for a while before going to the bar. He almost tucked them under the chair away from the man. Obviously, the man wanted him to be a drifter. Maybe he was a drifter. But not the kind the man wanted. The man's hands stroked Justin's calves and traveled up to his thighs.

"Do you want to take a shower?"

Justin locked himself in the bathroom. Music in the other room reached through the door. His hands shook. His body was no good. He was a disappointing lover, because he had never practiced. At his age, he would be expected to be proficient, but he needed guidance, wanted to ask for it. He tried not to think about all of the time he'd wasted being afraid of men, how he'd avoided finding himself in these situations. Why was he here now? He was tired. So exhausted he wanted to fall into someone's arms.

After the shower, he put his clothes back on his wet body and went out to the living room. The man had changed into sweats and a T-shirt. He sat in the leather chair, waiting.

"Shit," Justin said. "What's your name again? Did you tell me?"

"I told you," the man said, smiling with his mouth closed.

A voice floated out of the stereo. A high male voice. Pretty music with piano and violin. Not appropriate for what they were going to do. The apartment smelled newly of citrus. Justin's stomach ached from not eating. Could he ask for something to eat? The man's sweatpants bulged at the crotch.

"It's Bryan," the man said.

Yes, there it was. The name had been given to him at the bar, but there'd been so much going on in there. Bryan rose from the chair. Justin's heart skittered at the movement.

Bryan held him. Justin remembered to put his arms up and receive him and give something back. They ran their hands over each other, on the outsides of their clothes. Bryan kissed him on the corner of the mouth, and on the mouth fully, and Justin held him tighter. He slid his hand down to tentatively feel the bulge in Bryan's sweatpants. The last man he'd been with had been Nick. He hated to think about how pathetic it was, to have had one lover in his life, and for that person to have been Nick.

Bryan's hands went under Justin's shirt and explored his ribs and Justin almost pulled away. He did what the man did and tried to learn. He helped Bryan remove the shirt and sweatpants, took his own clothes off and left a pile of them on the carpet. It took so long to take off clothes, to work at it while someone was watching you. If only the lights would go out on their own, so he wouldn't have to ask for it.

They moved to the couch. Justin couldn't get hard again, his body clammy and cool. The man cupped his soft penis and kissed his neck, his ears, the middle of his chest, softly licked his nipples. Justin's body shook. Bryan was kind. He didn't get angry when Justin couldn't do what they had come here to do.

Part Three

THE LAKE MAN

They danced in the grass underneath the tent, strands of white lights twinkling above them. Willa stood with a clean plate in her hands that she had meant to fill with food and watched Justin with Shivam, whom she'd never met before. Justin hadn't told her anything about him or even that he had a boyfriend. He'd just brought Shivam to the wedding without a word. Not that she minded, but it had surprised her. The controlling part of her would have liked to have known, to have been able to prepare their mother, but no, Willa wanted that part of herself to die tonight. She was getting married. Everything felt new.

Justin was wearing nice clothes and holding someone in his arms. Over the last few months he'd created an attractive, serene person out of himself, the kind of person who could bring a date to his sister's wedding. What did Shivam know about Justin?

Shivam looked uncomfortable on the dance floor. Not quite ready to be stared at, or not at ease with himself enough to ignore everyone else. He was young and wolfish, his hair slicked. He wore thick-framed glasses that magnified his

eyes; one of them, she'd noticed earlier, was slightly lazy.
Instead of dress shoes he wore canvas sneakers with his suit.
He laughed, his teeth bright white and straight. Justin shut
his eyes now and then as they moved. Willa had known all
versions of her brother except this one. It had been over a
year since he'd arrived at her front door. He'd only moved
out three months ago.

She worried about Shivam's age. Next to Justin, he
looked like a teenager. It worried her because other people
were around, other people stared. Justin didn't deserve to
be stared at. Willa didn't want to know about her mother's
feelings on the subject. She wanted to be happy to see her
brother this way, before any complications arose.

On the tables, red cockscombs stood in vases like bloody
coral. The grass underfoot had flattened. "Weird flowers,"
her mother had said. But they'd been free, cut out of Luke's
mother's garden. Willa had wanted the wedding to be cheap
and small. She didn't want to be gawked at. She and Luke
were not "introduced" at the beginning of the reception.
They didn't dance while people watched. After the cere-
mony, everyone entered the tent to drink. Most of the people
here were Luke's family. Grace had insisted Willa invite her
aunt and cousins. She'd never been close with them, but she
was grateful they kept her mother busy, and they'd brought
money in cards.

At her table, Grace was also watching her son dance.
Willa wanted her mother to feel something about Justin
she'd never felt before. She should be pleased to see him
happy. He'd grown his hair long again, the scar on his head

invisible. He had gained some weight—the kind, Willa thought, that came with a new relationship.

One more glass of champagne and she would be drunk. Willa leaned on a table. A hand pressed into her back and she turned to find Jenny gently shoving her toward the dancers. Luke pulled his mother out into the grass and they did the same steps over and over. Moving quickly didn't come naturally to his mother, and it took her a few minutes to find the right rhythm. She stopped him and slipped her shoes off.

As the song changed, Jenny swung Willa around again and Justin broke away from Shivam and took Willa into his arms. Jenny snapped Shivam up. Willa didn't want anyone else to dance, and she tried to use a power inside her brain to keep the other guests seated. She imagined they'd all do this again sometime. She and Jenny and Justin and Shivam and Luke and his mother. Every year, they'd hold the anniversary of this dance.

"Aren't you something?" Willa said.

"Hm?" Justin said.

She remembered the time he'd stretched out on the roof of the old house and had let the sun burn him to a crisp. God, remember when he was vain? He'd worn cutoff shorts! He moved with her around the others and smiled at her. She rested her head on his shoulder, next to the scar on his neck. This person should not have a scar. He should not want to die young. When they neared Luke, he let her go and took Luke's mother in his arms and danced with her easily.

• •

As dinner wound down, Willa saw Grace talking to Justin, her hand on his arm. Justin rolled his eyes and rose from the table to follow their mother outside. Willa stood up quickly, making the plates and glasses clink. Luke met her eyes with concern.

It was hard to get through the huddles of guests when you were the reason everyone was there, but she made her way out and found Justin and their mother standing in the yard, the tent glowing behind them like a cocoon.

"He's a child," her mother said as she approached. Willa knew it was about Shivam.

"Don't say 'child' that way," Willa said.

"How can you be with that boy?" Grace said to Justin. "After what happened to you."

Justin's face wilted. "He's not a boy," he said. "He's twenty-three and he's the best person I know."

"That's what he told you. That he's twenty-three. I never imagined you'd become one of those men," Grace said. "I got used to the idea you'd be with men, but I never imagined this." She searched for a place to put her champagne glass down, but there was nothing around but grass. For acres, grass. They were using Luke's family's farm for the wedding. In the distance, a cow moaned. "What must these people think? How can you do this to your sister?"

"Oh, you got used to it, huh?" Justin said. "When did you get used to it?"

"Mom, shut up," Willa said. "Please stop."

"Tell me," Justin said. "What are these people thinking?"

"That you're a predator," she said. "You're a pedophile."

"Jesus Christ," Willa said. She covered her face so she wouldn't have to look at either of them. If Shivam had been a young woman, maybe Willa would have laughed, but she wouldn't have cringed as she had when she first saw Shivam with her thirty-five-year-old brother. Young men reminded her of children.

"You can't make me feel bad," Justin said.

"I need to go back," Willa said. But she didn't. She held Justin's arm. She wanted her mother to disappear, to just get in her car and leave. Shadows twirled inside the tent.

"He isn't a child," Justin said. "He's a man. If he were forty you would still hate it."

"Tell yourself whatever you want," their mother said. "You're with him because you're afraid of being with a grown-up. You don't have a real job and you're with this boy. I'm waiting for you to make one good decision."

"What would a good decision be? A woman?"

"Stop," Willa said. "That's enough. Let's go back, Justin."

Justin pulled his arm out of her grip. Willa didn't know the last time he'd seen Grace. She sensed an ending.

"You have no power," Justin said. He raised his hands with his palms facing their mother. Willa laughed. She felt Justin's drunkenness as he cursed Grace. His hands trembled.

"If you had tried harder you would have had a different life," Grace said. "He wouldn't have gotten you and hurt you. You're going to hurt this boy, too."

With his hands raised, he stepped forward and with a grunt shoved their mother into the grass. An arc of champagne hit Willa across the chest. Justin turned and walked back to the tent. Willa crouched to help Grace, but she rolled over and wept with her face in the lawn and squealed until partygoers peeked out of the opening of the tent to see what had happened.

The first night Shivam spent in Justin's apartment in Hudson, he walked around and examined Justin's possessions, picked up books and put them aside after reading the first pages. It was a few weeks before Willa's wedding, and they were both rumpled in their sleep clothes. Shivam had borrowed pajama pants from Justin, which were too long. He rubbed the hair on his chest and stood in front of a framed botanical print Willa had given Justin.

"I like this," Shivam said. "Milkweed."

With another person here, Justin understood how the apartment must look, with a little of this and that strewn around. He didn't have his own taste. The botanical print was Willa's taste. She'd given it to him and he liked it enough to put on the wall. He hoarded books and piled them up, until he got around to organizing and reading them. Mythology, fantasy, fairy tales, dramas, science fiction.

Shivam was getting his master of arts in teaching at Bard College. Justin tried to picture him in his jeans and combat boots standing in front of a classroom full of teenagers someday, teaching them biology.

"You're too young for me," Justin said. He'd been

silently panicking as Shivam wandered the apartment. They had met at work at the community college. Justin had seen Shivam around the administration building on and off before they met. Shivam worked a summer job in one of the offices.

"You say that a lot," Shivam said.

Did he? He didn't like to repeat himself, but he often did. Willa was always telling him. With her, he got angry, but it embarrassed him to do it in front of Shivam.

"What are you nervous about?" Shivam said. "You're not doing anything wrong."

• •

At work, Justin was known as the person who made mistakes, but his coworkers were gentle with him, because he'd become the office confidant. He worked with women in their late fifties and early sixties, who all had family dramas. Their cell phones rang throughout the day, and he listened to their voices floating over the cubicles, arguing with their grown children. They stopped at his desk and talked about their daughters' wedding plans, their sons' illnesses or arrests. He listened and wanted to solve their problems, but he offered no advice or solutions. He was a mess, but none of them knew it. Maybe.

He had become a civil servant after taking a test a ten-year-old could've passed. He had health insurance for the first time in his adult life but made little money to start and could only afford a studio apartment. He worked with other people who had not gone to college, either. They toiled in a basement filled with long black file cabinets and the constant roar of the HVAC system. Hundreds of young people called the office and he spoke to many of them, listening to their anxiety and excitement. They were demanding and impatient. They bore no resemblance to himself or anyone he'd known as a teenager. Many of the boys barely enunciated their words. Parents often asked if he was a student himself, implying a grown man should not be answering phones in an admissions office. These were parents who were slightly older than himself. "No," he told them. "This is my job."

His coworkers were used to his limitations and his habits, though he frustrated them. He heard the women talking about him when they thought he was out of range. "I've showed him a billion times how to do it, and he does it right the first few times and then messes it up again."

God, he hated to be wrong. He hated to be a fuckup, but he was used to it. Post-it notes with scribbled reminders decorated his computer and desk. The women weren't cruel. They were blowing off steam, but he wished they'd come to him, remind him, correct him, instead of talking to each other about him.

On his break, he met Shivam for a walk. He understood they might look strange together. He, tall and scrawny, with gray hairs in his beard, and Shivam more than two heads shorter, dressed in street clothes despite the fact that he was also working. Shivam wore T-shirts for punk bands Justin had never heard of. Half a mile from the administration buildings, behind the baseball field, there was a small lake with a track circling it. It was a reminder of what had been here before the campus had been built. Wetlands and woods. Large old trees bent at the water's edge. Shivam pointed out native plants. Ironweed, boneset, bee balm, Joe-Pye weed. Red-winged blackbirds gripped the long reeds and whistled.

Justin hadn't expected to meet anyone of interest at work. Shivam surprised him and reached for his hand, and Justin wouldn't let him take it.

"It's fine," Shivam said.

"I don't like PDA," Justin said.

They weren't in public. There were no witnesses. He felt young and stupid, not at all the grown man who woke in the morning with an aching lower back from sleeping on a mattress on the floor. He rubbed Shivam's forearm and liked the feel of his skin. He'd never been ashamed of being gay, no matter how hard his mother had tried to shame him. It wasn't that. He didn't want to be afraid of Shivam, but he was.

Shivam led him off the path and leaned him against a tree. Somewhere in the distance, people were talking. Shivam undid Justin's pants and put his hand inside.

"I think you're beautiful," Shivam said.

Justin's face prickled with sweat. "I'm not. Please stop."

Shivam pulled his hand out of Justin's pants.

"I'm sorry," Justin said.

"No, it's all right. We shouldn't do this out here."

He wasn't fun enough. Shivam would meet someone his own age, and Justin would be something he'd tried out. Justin fastened the button at the top of his pants and zipped himself up.

• •

Over the past year, Justin had started caring more about how he dressed, about keeping himself together. He wanted to show Willa he knew how to take care of himself without her help. When he moved out, she texted him all the time, asked if he needed anything, if she should come help him get settled. She didn't know why he had to move to Hudson, almost an hour away from her, but he wanted to try again to make a life for himself, and it was already better than when he'd moved to Albany on his own.

He made an effort to be attractive for Shivam but he worried he would see through him, would sense what was rotten inside him, so he tried hard to hide it. He said yes when Shivam asked him to do things he would normally avoid: go to a crowded club to see a loud band play, meet Shivam and his friends at a restaurant. He'd done this three weeks into dating Shivam. The friends seemed much younger than Shivam, and it was disconcerting. Justin was out of his element and didn't understand many of their references.

He got his hair cut every four weeks now and kept it longish, but neat. He trimmed his beard himself, staring into the bathroom mirror with a buzzing device at his neck. He ran most mornings by the river, worked out for free at the gym on campus among the young, beautiful, intimidating jocks. He remembered to smile and decided it would be best not to talk too much, but listen to Shivam talk. When Shivam asked him questions about what he'd done before coming to Hudson, before working at the college, he didn't lie, but omitted.

"I lived in my hometown and worked," he said. "Spent time with my family."

He realized he'd forgotten to think about what he really wanted. In the past, he'd tried writing, but he couldn't focus. He had trouble reading. How would he write? He told Shivam he wanted to, as it was better to have something you wanted to do besides your little office job, though he stressed to Shivam that he enjoyed his little office job, too; he didn't require money or status, wanted to live simply.

If Shivam didn't stay over, Justin didn't sleep. When he was around Shivam he forgot to what extent he was hiding; the other Justin became real but fell away when he was alone, and it frightened him how much he wanted to be with Shivam, how much he wanted to always live inside the other person he was when Shivam was around.

Willa and Luke had slept in. After the wedding they had dragged themselves upstairs to a guest room in his parents' house. Sometime in the very early morning, Willa had woken up and opened the window. Now the morning air flowed in along with the sounds of relentless birdsong and the cows on the farm across the road. Willa took a shower without waking Luke and went downstairs.

Luke's mother, Sue, was in the kitchen, eating a bowl of cereal with slices of browning banana on top. The smell of the banana hit Willa and she backed away from it and stood at the counter. She hadn't felt hungover until this moment. She filled a glass with water.

After the reception, Sue had brought Grace into the house and insisted she also stay over. Willa had almost clawed at her own face with embarrassment. Her mother, in her drunkenness, wept openly. "I'm so sorry," she said as tears streamed into her mouth, "but my son and I had a fight. He can be cruel. I don't know if Willa has explained to you—he has emotional problems."

Emotional problems? Her mother had her own story

about Justin. Willa wanted to confront her, but not in front of Sue.

Out the kitchen window, the tent still stood in the field waiting for the rental company to come take it down. Luke's father, who had probably been awake since dawn, appeared from behind the tent, a black trash bag in his hands.

"Your mother was in a much better mood this morning," Sue said. "She drove herself home."

"She doesn't usually drink," Willa said. She hated her habit of defending her mother. Justin called her on it all the time, and he was right. Grace didn't need defending, but it came so naturally to Willa.

"Weddings are emotional," Sue said. "Families, you know?"

From the beginning, Willa had experienced Sue's kindness with suspicion, but she was growing accustomed to it. Sue continued eating and didn't seem uneasy, not the way Willa did.

• •

Willa sat by an open window at her mother's. The neighbor kids played in the yard. The older girl seemed to be filming the two young boys with her phone as they pretended to do martial arts. "Sue is a nice woman," Grace said. She placed a cup of black coffee in front of Willa.

"Yes, she is," Willa said. "I'm lucky."

They were quiet a long time, and Willa thought about

saying everything she'd wanted to say last night. To explode. *You embarrassed me! You were the cruel one, and you don't see it.*

"I was so hurt," Grace said. "You wouldn't stand up for me. You know, I'm only trying to keep him from making another mistake."

"I wish you could see yourself," Willa said. "When you think you're helping."

"That's what you think? I'm glad to know it. I can never do anything right for either of you," Grace said. "I know, I wasn't enough for you. I wasn't your father. I knew how much you wanted me to take over for him."

"No. I didn't," Willa said.

"You were always disappointed. You needed so much and I wasn't good enough. And your brother. Try to put yourself in my shoes for once. Remember what he put us through with his moods and his meanness and doing whatever he was doing with that man. He ruined us. I couldn't leave the house without being stared at and talked about for what he did. As if it were my fault. He killed a child. He brought pain to our house. Worse than when your father died."

"He didn't," Willa said. "Don't say that. He didn't kill a child."

"He might as well have. And now. Showing up with a boy at your wedding. He did it on purpose."

"He is not a boy."

"That may be a fact, but it doesn't matter. When people looked at them, they saw a man and a boy. I can't take it. I can't take how he deliberately makes these choices. Aren't you embarrassed? Weren't you when you were a girl? Don't lie to me. I know how you were treated in school."

"I didn't come here to talk about this," Willa said, though she had. It was too overwhelming now. She wanted to be home in bed with Luke. She wanted to move with him to Santa Fe or Boston or Portland, Oregon, and pretend they didn't have families. Why had she gotten out of bed on the morning after her wedding to try to fix this?

"Why did you come here? To yell at me?" her mother said.

"I don't remember," Willa said. Outside, one of the kids screeched as if witnessing a murder. Willa put her freezing hand on her mother's and played with the ring Grace wore. The engagement ring Arthur had given her in 1978. "I wish you could forgive him," Willa said.

• •

In the car, she called Luke.

"I woke up and thought it was five years into the future and we were divorced," he said.

"I'm at my mother's."

"How is she this morning?"

"Fine. Your mother probably thinks we're dysfunctional."

"You are dysfunctional," Luke said.

"But I didn't want her to know that."

"She loves you," he said.

Willa wasn't comfortable thinking of Luke's mother's

love. It didn't belong to her. She had her own mother. Luke's family, their sprawling, beautiful property, their good-natured conversation, all of it delighted and annoyed her. Luke's family ate the same kinds of foods and rarely strayed, watched sports or the news, never movies. For exercise, Sue and her husband walked the property holding hands. It was just so foreign. Someday, Willa would be able to accept Sue loving her. Or she never would, and she'd have to keep faking it.

She told Luke she was coming home, but instead of heading back to the apartment, she drove to the thruway. If she called Justin and told him she was coming, he'd tell her to stay away. When he answered the door, he didn't look surprised to see her, and before he closed it and came out into the hall, he glanced once behind him. She was certain Shivam was asleep inside. Did he not want her to know this?

They went for a walk in the neighborhood, past old, bright-colored buildings on the main street. Few people were out so early on a Saturday. At the end of the nineteenth century, Hudson had been known for its bars and broth-els. "We're living on vice street," Justin told her. "Sailors stopped here and had sex and got wasted."

They walked to the park at the river's edge and sat on a pitted bench.

"Aren't you supposed to have a husband now?" Justin said.

"I left him at home," she said. "I didn't tell him where I was going."

"You're not good at this."

"He was all right. After I called him."

On the way to the park, Justin had bought two doughnuts. He handed her one and pulled his own apart and ate it a piece at a time.

"I saw a bald eagle here last week," he told her.

"Really?"

"I've been coming every day to try and catch it again, but I haven't been lucky."

She loved to sit in the sun with her brother. She almost told him how wonderful she felt.

"So why did you come?" he said.

It hurt to hear the accusation in his voice. She had never visited him here before. He must have smelled their mother on her. "You don't want to talk about what happened at the wedding?"

"I'm sorry," he said. "I shouldn't have . . ."

Before she took a breath, he snapped.

"What the fuck am I talking about? I'm not sorry." He dropped half a doughnut into the dirt. "You should be sorry."

"Me? I didn't do anything," she said. "You pushed our mother onto the ground."

"Yes, you're right. You didn't do anything. You didn't try to stick up for me. You never have."

"I did try," she said. She remembered trying, having the feeling of trying.

"You told her to stop. But you didn't tell her that what she was saying was garbage. You didn't tell her she was wrong. She doesn't seem to know. It would mean something from you, Willa. It means nothing coming from me. The reason you don't is that part of you agrees with her."

How could he think this? Hadn't she been there to take him in when he needed her? Willa tried to search for the truth in what he'd said, to see herself as clearly as possible. Her eyes burned, the sun closer and hotter.

Even before Nick, Justin was always blaming. He'd seen her as a traitor when they were kids. Because she wanted their mother to love her. "Take some responsibility for what you did. At my wedding!"

"Let me guess," he said. "You were over there before you came here. What were you going to do? Try to talk me into forgiving her for calling me a fucking pedophile? The two of you belong together."

"She doesn't know what she's saying," Willa said. "I know it was wrong. This isn't about Shivam."

"I hate that," he said. "You can't pretend it has nothing to do with him."

A jogger passed and kicked gravel. Willa imagined she'd switched places with him and was running along the river with a metallic breeze cooling her face.

"If she wants to be angry at me forever, she can do it at the bottom of a well," Justin said.

It was outrageous, to be criticized by him, after she'd stood by him all these years, after she had held his blood in her hands, trying to press it back into his body. "It's all about what happened to you. You never asked me what it was like for me."

The old anger returned. He should know how much

anger she'd kept inside her, afraid to send it in his direction, worried he couldn't handle it. Always worried about his feelings.

"People hated me. When you were gone, someone broke into the house and pissed in the living room. Did you know that? Kids threw rocks at our windows. You never noticed how scared we were. You never said you were sorry."

Red blotches appeared on Justin's neck and cheeks as if she'd slapped him.

She panicked and tried to rewind. "No," she said. "I know it wasn't your fault. My brain knows."

"When the rest of you knows it, give me a call."

From the bench, she watched him walk away until he'd grown small and disappeared around a corner. She turned to the giant, polluted river. In the winter, thick sheets of ice would break into slabs and crash over each other at the shore.

She'd wait a few days and call him. He'd forgive her for saying the wrong things, because he must know she was on his side. Before heading back to the car, she stopped in a bakery and bought a baguette, which she tore and ate as she walked and continued to break apart in the car, chewing and chewing and swallowing the dry pieces. A gob of bread got stuck in her throat and she lost control of the car a little. She worked the bread down her esophagus, moved into the slow lane. She wasn't choking. Not really. It just hurt.

Shivam wanted to get away from his apartment, where he'd been living with a straight couple, both friends of his. Their relationship had begun to wear on him. They'd started using him in their fights. He found a one-bedroom house for rent on the edge of a lake an hour north of Albany. Calling it a house was a stretch. It was a shack, but there was a bathroom, running water he didn't quite trust, and a woodstove for cold nights. The rent was cheap enough for him to afford to stay for a month before having to go home and secure a job for the rest of the summer.

Shivam talked Justin into taking a full two weeks off at the end of July, and they drove to the lake house together. When they arrived, they carried their bags into the house and opened the windows to air the place out. It smelled of fish and rainwater. The humidity was oppressive inside and out. Shivam stripped off his clothes. He walked around freely, standing in front of the sliding doors that led onto the rickety deck facing the water. The house was nestled in a small cove. Trees protected it on both sides. Across the lake stood beautiful houses where rich white people vacationed; their children bobbed and shriveled in the water.

• •

In the afternoon, Shivam put on a bathing suit and swam out to the small island, not far from the shore. The man he'd rented the house from told him it was called Christmas Tree Island because of the single old evergreen that lived there. Boats tooled around. Voices vibrated nearby. He loved to swim but was out of practice, so by the time he reached the island, he crawled out of the water and lay in the dirt for ten minutes. The remnants of old campfires decorated the beach. Amber bottles lay whole and broken in the grass. The island was covered in scrub and Queen Anne's lace, coneflowers, and blue chicory.

Shivam's parents now spent their summers traveling around the country. His brother and two sisters were scattered, working, going to school, or having babies. He was the youngest and doing fine, so no one bothered him much. His mother called him twice a week, and he tried to check in with his father via email. He hadn't told them about Justin, but not out of shame. To bring him up would lead to questions Shivam didn't want to answer. He loved his parents, but his mother could be relentless when it came to sniffing out the particulars of his personal life.

Recently, he'd outright lied to her, saying he was not seeing anyone. He told himself he wanted to keep Justin a secret for as long as possible. That way, their relationship would feel like his own thing, protected from criticism. He wanted to enjoy it and be brainless and happy for a while. He feared his parents' reaction to Justin's age, his job and lack of degree, the fact that he wasn't Indian. He put all of these pressures on himself. They hadn't done it to him. He wanted to please them so badly, he imagined that any choice he made might be the one that lost him their favor. His mother had surprised him before. When he'd been panicked, in terror, telling her he was gay, she had shaken him slightly. "Why do you assume to know how I'll react? Stop crying."

Mosquitoes landed on his neck and sucked. He was stupid to come out here alone. He sat upright with his feet in the water and looked back at the house, which was farther away than he'd expected. Justin came out onto the deck. Shivam waved, but Justin didn't see him.

Earlier, they'd fooled around in the main room with sun coming through the sliding doors. Justin had attacked him, as if he had never seen Shivam's body before. Maybe it was the humidity turning them on? Justin wasn't always so enthusiastic. After, they lay there laughing at how silent it was in the house. Laughing at their own quick breathing and mouth noises.

Sometimes Justin's soul left the room, his body a quiet shell. The last time it happened, Shivam pulled the short hairs of Justin's beard and Justin squealed back to reality with tears popping in his eyes. They hadn't talked about it.

Back at the house, Justin hurried from the deck and onto the grass, where he stood for a while. Shivam walked out a bit into the lake and scared the minnows. The sun flashed on them. Coins of an underwater city. Shivam swam away from the island. He'd been doing so much sitting around with books or at the computer. He hadn't been using his muscles for anything. His shoulders burned as he pushed through the water.

"Hello there!" Justin's voice called.

But Shivam didn't have the breath to yell. He needed all of it to make it back. Justin's skin appeared and disappeared, standing out against the green of the grass and the shabby gray house. Shivam went under and the weed-flecked, gritty world below the surface clouded his view. The next time he came up for air, Justin had disappeared from the beach.

Maybe he'd gone inside or around the front of house, thinking Shivam was fine. Shivam closed his eyes and imagined himself pushing forward, reaching the shore. Something bumped against his shoulder. A lake monster. An ancient carp or something. But no, it was Justin. Justin had dived in and swum out. Shivam let himself rest on Justin's cool, tacky body. Foam decorated Justin's beard and there were leaves in his hair.

"I'm not the best swimmer," he said.

"Me neither," Shivam said. "I was stupid."

Justin tugged them both in the direction of the house. At the shore, they crawled into the grass and lay there. Shivam hoped no one had witnessed their pathetic struggle. Humiliated and sore, he put his hand on Justin's chest and felt his heart.

"Let's make a rule to never do that without the other person," Justin said.

Justin often seemed younger than him. It didn't bother Shivam, but it entered his mind. Maybe you were always the same; only your body grew and changed. Justin, who was thirty-five, didn't remind Shivam of any other thirty-something people. Justin took his hand and held it. "You looked like you were swimming in slow motion," he said.

• •

"You basically saved my life," Shivam said. He was enjoying embarrassing Justin, inflating what had happened to them. "You're a hero."

"I think we saved each other," Justin said. He laughed, but he was growing in his swim trunks. "I wouldn't know how to tell that story."

Shivam gripped him gently through the material. "I'll tell it," he said. "I'll tell everyone I know you saved me."

"Stop it." Shivam picked leaves out of Justin's hair. They both smelled like the lake. The sun, unobscured by clouds, warmed them.

A bird—Shivam couldn't tell what it was from here—landed on the water and dived under. It stayed submerged for a long time, and they watched the water, waiting for it to reappear. When it did, he saw it was a grebe, its small red eye needling him.

Justin lay on a towel now. "I'd like to live here and be odd. I'll become a hermit the lake kids'll be afraid of, and I'll have no family. I'll never speak to Willa again, but she won't miss me. I won't have anyone. My face'll turn leathery."

"You don't want to talk to Willa anymore? Why not?" Shivam had liked Willa. At the wedding, she'd danced with him, a little drunk, but he could tell she meant it when she told him she was happy he was there, happy he was with Justin.

"I don't really want that," Justin said. He went quiet for a long time.

Shivam put his arm over his eyes to block the sun. It was torture, waiting to trust someone. Did Justin really want to be completely alone? *Without me?* Shivam wanted to say. *Even me?* You had to be so careful. People got scared away.

"Let's be hermits together," Shivam said.

"Yes," Justin said, and Shivam's muscles released with gratitude.

L ate at night, Justin woke in the dark in the bedroom, certain a man had been standing at the foot of the bed. Beside him, Shivam breathed. Someone had opened the door to
the room. He had closed it himself and now it was open. He
sat and tucked his feet under himself. There was no one. He
searched the bed next to him and caressed Shivam's hairy arm
and shoulder and heard him question with a noise. He took
his hand back. He wouldn't wake Shivam. No one had been
here. It was in his head, a dream that had followed him out of
sleep. Shivam could have left the door open after using the
bathroom in the night. Justin felt his way through the cabin to
the sliding doors. Even with all the windows shut, the sound
of night insects and tree frogs invaded. A shape hulked in the
dark ahead of him. He turned on the lamp on the table next
to the rotting old couch. At the glass doors, a man stood half
in and half out, unmoved by the light. Wet hair lay in weedy
clumps around his forehead and over his ears, and his eyes
were like a bird's after it has flown into a window.

Justin's hands went to his own heart. He'd expected to
attack if ever confronted, to scream, but he was too afraid
to save himself or Shivam.

The man's feet were streaked with mud and he wore only a bathing suit, goggles pushed up onto his head, his body scrawny and hairless, pale, his nipples pink. Water splattered off him and onto the floor.

"Who are you?" Justin said. "Get out of here."

The man slid gently through the doors and onto the deck and lingered there. Justin hurried to the door and closed and locked it. The man had nothing in his hands. He walked as if he couldn't remember where he wanted to go. Down the stairs and into the yard, where his pale skin glowed in the moonlight.

A fire grew under Justin's arms and across his face. The man disappeared into the dark and Justin's feet unglued from the floor. He waited for several minutes, breathed on the glass, went out and down the steps from the deck and into the grass, which soaked his feet.

The lake was so still, he imagined if he stepped onto it, he would be held, and he'd be able to walk to the island. He couldn't see it, but it was there, a hump on the water. A beast rising, with a mossy horn, the old tree. He sensed something lived there. In this dark, it was easy to pretend he didn't have a body. Why had it been so hard for Shivam to swim there and back? A young, strong man.

Out there something splashed in the water, either diving in or turning over. Large enough that it sent the water lapping at the shore by his feet. He hurried back into the house and locked the sliding doors.

For the rest of the night, Justin sat on the couch. He realized how foolish he was being. The man, whoever he was, hadn't tried to hurt them. Maybe he'd been a sleepwalker. Or maybe he hadn't been real. He hated to think it. Justin had smelled the lake; coolness coming off the man's body had caressed his face. Even if he wanted to sleep, he wouldn't be able to, thinking about the man's empty, startled eyes.

In the morning, Shivam came out and joined him. "How long have you been out here?"

"A little while," Justin said. "An hour, I guess."

"Oh. I had a weird sleep. I kept waking up and noticing you were gone."

"No. I was there."

G*ood morning, sweetheart. You're in a safe place.* Here was a light in his eyes, one on the right, one on the left. *Can you tell us your name?* someone coaxed him. Justin lay in a bed in a white space, a small room only large enough for a few people to fit inside. There were chairs against the wall, but no one sat in them. Only he and the woman next to him existed.

Days and days ago, or yesterday, or last week, or months ago, he'd woken up in the woods. He couldn't remember how he'd gotten there. In an in-between time, not day or night, the dog visited him. The dog from the town full of old men. It breathed on him, on his neck and wet face, and licked his hands. Above them a bird sat on a tree branch and screeched, a noise like a door opening in an old house. The bird's eyes looked in two directions at once. It clicked its beak and screeched again. The screech painted the forest with frost. It flew away with silent wings.

He sat up and fell, then dragged himself in the easiest direction, down a slight incline. A road or water gleamed on the other side of the trees. He remembered. He'd come from there. He had been with Nick.

A woman sat next to his bed. The woman wiped his face with a damp cloth. She asked him more questions and the questions made him sweat with exertion.

"You have been in this hospital for three weeks. You were hit on the head and had surgery. You were unconscious and on a ventilator. But you're doing much better now. It's okay," she said. "It's okay." She comforted, though he didn't cry. He tried to examine himself, but he had been covered. He wanted to ask the woman questions. She wouldn't know the answers. He understood he couldn't ask Nick because Nick was gone.

It had been cold in the woods, the sound of a car going by periodically. He saw he'd done something to himself without realizing or remembering; he'd taken leaves and whatever else from the ground and placed them over his body.

"Nick," he said to the woman.

"You're lucky to be alive, Nick," the woman said.

Someone saw him. A truck halted in the road. It must be Nick, though Nick didn't drive a truck. A figure got out and approached him. How much time had passed? Justin couldn't lift any part of himself. His eyes wanted to close.

"Are you alive?" a man shouted. "Can you hear me? Are you alive?"

Ha, he said. Just a breath sound. The man took off his coat and threw it over him; the man spoke to himself in a low voice. *Oh god. Jesus. Okay. Okay.* The smell of cigarettes and mint gum eased over his face. He'd never been comforted by those smells before, but he loved them now and wanted to sleep.

"Stay here," the man said, and a rough hand rested on his arm. "Don't go anywhere." Of course, he would stay. "Keep your eyes on me." He saw a beard and a neck. The man unpeeled him from the ground and he fell away again into darkness. "Don't sleep!" When he awoke, the wind rushed by his face, going fast. A rough blanket around him, and the stars appeared, at least he thought they were stars; sparks flew over the roof of the truck.

Justin told Shivam he was going to town to shop for groceries. First, he drove around the lake once, looking out the window at the houses visible from the road. It was a useless activity. He pulled the car over onto a patch of dead grass under some evergreens, got out, and walked along the road until he spotted a quiet house with dark windows. Fresh tire tracks gouged the mud and gravel along the side of the house. He trotted down a hill and into the grass, where someone had left a small fiberglass boat. He pushed it to the water and fell into it, almost capsizing.

He took the single oar and swept it through the water, made his way slowly around the lake until his arms grew tired. He floated. In the distance, their cabin appeared empty, though Shivam was inside it. A boat with music playing on it went by and someone shouted at him. The water humped and he held on to the sides of his little boat until it was flat again.

He wouldn't find the lake man, but he watched the swimmers, or the people at the shore. When he regained strength, he oared the boat in the direction of Christmas Tree Island and watched their cabin grow larger. He plunged the oar into the water and instead of cutting through easily, it knocked into something, a long, pale figure swimming fast. The figure continued to swim under the surface, and Justin held the oar up out of the water. He waited for the swimmer to come up for air, but it never did.

When he got back to the cabin, Shivam hurried to him. He must have looked insane, disheveled.

"You stink!" Shivam said, making a funny whooping noise at Justin's BO. "Where's the food? What happened?"

"Nothing," Justin said. "I guess I forgot."

"You forgot you were going to the store?"

"I got distracted. I can go now, though, if you really want me to."

"I don't want you to, it was your idea in the first place. It's just weird you didn't go."

"I can go," Justin said. His anger revved, and he didn't know why. "If you want me to go, just say it."

"Why are you acting like this?" Shivam said. "What happened?"

"Nothing happened," Justin said. "I'm going to go to the store now. I meant to. We don't have to talk about it anymore. I'm going."

He stood; his arms were heavy.

"Sit down," Shivam said. "You're being a weirdo."

Justin walked out of the cabin and up the gravel driveway to the street, but the car wasn't there. He'd left it under the evergreens somewhere on the other side of the lake.

• •

Shivam wasn't thinking clearly. He was already in love with Justin, though he didn't say this aloud to Justin or anyone else. He would deal with whatever came, and it would probably hurt him. You couldn't avoid being hurt.

Inside the cabin, Justin slept, or said he was going to try. The sun blazed. Shivam took off his shirt and jumped into the water to cool off; he wouldn't be swimming to Christmas Tree Island again on his own. He swished around for a bit in the cool lake, climbed out, and lay on a towel in the grass. A radio played bad radio music a few houses away. All popular music did for him was make him sleepy. He liked to be in a sweaty crowd with knives of distorted guitar slicing through him from a stage.

His friends, who'd met Justin only once, were skeptical. Justin seemed off, they said, and Shivam defended him, told them to mind their business, but he'd asked them what they thought, and they'd told him. Justin's body delighted him, the soft muscle of his chest and upper arms, his hairy legs and stomach, how he kissed softly and then with concentration, his tongue playing against Shivam's. At first, his interest in Justin had been primarily physical. He loved Justin's penis, the smooth curve of it, and how it fit nicely in his hand. The taste and smell of Justin, his sweat. And he was kind and worried about being insensitive. They could be quiet together.

The argument about the grocery store worried him. Justin had left to go to the store and had come back with nothing and no explanation. He wasn't sleeping at night, though he lied to Shivam and said he was. There were conversations they needed to have that they weren't having. Shivam wanted to know about the scars on Justin's body, places where he'd been opened and sewn up again, but didn't want anything to change, didn't want to scare Justin.

If they lived at the lake house away from the world, from friends who didn't approve, from Justin's family, they'd be silent and in love. They wouldn't need conversations or history or the future. Shivam would be happy to lay his head on Justin's stomach, to smell his smell, to lick his armpits, to fuck him. When they had sex, Justin appeared relieved. When they kissed and removed their clothes, Justin shivered, a fear briefly falling over his face until Shivam couldn't stop himself from kissing him to make it disappear.

The first time they had sex, Justin had been tentative. They'd been together a few times before, but had only kissed and jerked each other off.

They were on Justin's bed in the dark, a yellow light coming through the windows. "Are you sure you want me to?" Justin said.

Shivam's calves were on Justin's shoulders. He enjoyed the look of them framing Justin's face. They had already talked about what they would do. Yes, he wanted it. Justin had put on the condom and slicked himself and Shivam with lubricant and took a long time trying to get inside him, and once he did, he lay on top of Shivam, gently moving in and out. The brief pain melted and warmth radiated into Shivam's stomach. He pulled Justin close to him. He sometimes left himself when he was being fucked, wanted to forget his life and his name, to be whatever he was feeling with another person inside him. With Justin, he wanted to be himself, to remember the feeling of pleasure building as he stroked himself, becoming almost uncontrollable. Justin was giving it to him. Shivam groaned in his ear and asked him to go harder. With his hands, he moved Justin's head so he could look at his eyes.

"Is it good?" Justin said.

"Yes," Shivam told him.

Shivam grabbed him by his ears and brought his face close to kiss his mouth. Justin came quickly as they kissed and slid out of Shivam. He waited for Justin to say or do something, but it was taking too long, so he sat and looked at him lying on his back, his penis soft and tired. Sweat curled the hair on his chest a bit. Shivam ran his hands over Justin's arms and legs, his torso, his face, as if performing some kind of ritual.

"I never liked it," Justin said.

"Not everyone does," Shivam said. He hoped Justin would say why he didn't like it. He sensed there was a reason other than preference.

"But you do," Justin said.

"Yes, I do," Shivam said. "With you especially."

"I don't know what I'm doing. I'm no good at it."

"You are. I loved it." *I love you*, he meant to say. *I want to always be doing this with you.*

"Will you try it with me?" Justin said. "But if I can't, we have to stop."

"Of course," Shivam said.

Justin, silent and breathing, his eyes open; he watched

everything Shivam did. Shivam pumped lubricant onto his fingers, he put one finger inside Justin, and then another. He took his time, now and then bending to kiss Justin's thigh, his stomach, to suck him as he eased his finger in and out. They moved together in the quiet. "Am I hurting you? Don't be afraid to tell me," Shivam said.

"No," Justin said. "The opposite."

Shivam watched his face, the slow transformation in his eyes. He worried he was forcing this, but after a time, Justin's face changed. He was enjoying it. Shivam pressed himself against him, his chest against Justin's, and they stayed locked that way for a while, not moving, until Justin's lips brushed Shivam's ear. "Okay," he said.

By the end of the second week, Justin wanted to leave the lake, but it was hard. He'd started to think the quiet wasn't good for him. At night, he fell asleep and awoke with his heart pounding an hour or so later, fell asleep again and awoke again with his heart pounding.

He had a secret now. The man from the lake. He hadn't told Shivam about him; he wasn't certain it had been real. In his mind, the lake man rocketed through the water, never coming to the surface for air, on his way back to the cabin.

They were both grouchy as they loaded the car. Earlier, they'd gone swimming and had cooked hot dogs on the grill and sat in the grass to eat them. Some of the children a few houses away floated by in a canoe and waved at them. No one spoke to them, but people knew who they were. Two weeks is a long time; people get used to you quickly. Maybe they would come back here every year and people would feel happy to recognize them.

The nurses and doctors had found nothing on him. Whatever he did have had slipped away from him, had fallen out of his pockets or had been taken away. The man who'd brought him here had left before anyone could find out who he was. They discovered a report of a missing boy with the name Justin Dunham. They told him the name and it was his. A woman came to see him. It had been a long, unbroken day. People going in and out. Someone woke him. Let him sleep. Woke him. The woman was his mother.

A nurse came in with her and helped her and he watched them talking about him. He said, "Hello."

She sat by him and put a hand on his hand. He remembered the touch, the way an image from a dream comes to you, but you've forgotten it was a dream. An image that flashes and switches on something inside you. The landscape of her palm, dry and soft, on top of his own skin. And there was the feeling of the ring, a little hard, cool slip of metal. Her hand rested on him and he looked at it for a while.

• •

When he and Shivam returned from the lake, the work waiting for him in the office overwhelmed him. He'd never been
away for so long. One of his coworkers, Kate, visited him
in his cubicle to explain how she'd helped him while he was
away, but she had her own work, too. Her husband, she told
him, had fallen down the stairs a week ago, so she'd been
out caring for him. As she spoke, he focused on the ribbon
of emails in his inbox and the papers next to his keyboard.

"I'm sorry," he said. "Is he okay?"

She put her hand on the stack of files on his desk. "He
was hurt," she said, and started to cry. Other people's tears
embarrassed him, and she wept openly. He cried often, but it
always surprised him when other people did it.

She was a nice woman, and he'd known her now for a
year, but he wasn't prepared to comfort her. His office friendships were one-sided. He shared nothing with anyone, but
he laughed at his coworkers' jokes and listened to their problems. Now he folded his hands in his lap and waited for Kate
to finish crying. She wiped at her tears, and he stood and let
her sit in his chair. When she stopped crying, he had an idea.

She followed him out of the office and they walked
away from the building and across to a stand of trees where
he'd once seen woodpeckers excavating. He'd read somewhere that being near trees reduced stress, and he told her
this. A calm rushed through him as a breeze sent old willow
branches sweeping against the pavement.

• •

Willa had never called him on his work phone before. He wished he could take the phone out in the hall. In this office, everyone listened to everyone else's personal calls. "I tried calling your cell fifty times," said Willa. "I'm sorry you have to talk to me. I got the hint. But I thought you'd want to know. Mrs. Flores died."

Justin hadn't seen René since before Willa's wedding. He'd gone a handful of times after moving out of Willa's apartment, confronting Brianna, who still hated him. He'd sat with René while Brianna stood in the doorway watching. His visits had done nothing for René, hadn't brought her comfort, so he stopped going. When once they'd enjoyed some kind of connection, on those visits he sensed indifference. He understood. Why should he mean anything to her when she was leaving so soon?

"Are you there?" Willa said.

"Yes," he said. "I'll go with you. If there's a funeral or something."

"I'm sorry," Willa said.

• •

That Friday, he took the train to Poughkeepsie and Willa picked him up and they drove into New Paltz together. As they drove over the Mid-Hudson Bridge, he remembered René was dead. Since he'd gotten home from the lake, he hadn't slept. Instead of falling asleep and waking during the night, he lay in bed with his eyes open, and in the dark over his bed, he saw the lake man, pale and glowing. In the morning he splashed cold water on his face to revive himself.

Willa didn't ask where he'd been or why she hadn't been able to get in touch with him. She barely spoke. She turned the radio on and one of their favorite songs came on. It was called "Don't You Want Me?" and Willa sang the man's part. She made her voice low and used an English accent. When the woman's part came on, Justin sang, also with an accent, though his wasn't as good as Willa's. He laughed and missed lines. When the song ended, they didn't talk, but listened to the radio until they arrived at the funeral home.

Justin stood in the hall outside the viewing room, looking in at the crowd and René's casket. Willa walked around the room.

"I think it's all right for you to go in," she said when she found him again.

Brianna was too distraught to care about Justin. He'd put on a nice shirt and the only pair of dress pants he owned. Some people were dressed elegantly in black. One man wore shorts with a polo shirt tucked into them. On each side of the casket, arrangements of white lilies guarded René. Brianna stood in the corner of the room with a little girl next to her. She talked to a man, who nodded as she spoke. From here, her eyes looked dry and red, cried out. Justin wouldn't approach her.

Willa took his arm, and he gently pulled it away from her and walked into the room and down the aisle to the casket. Inside lay a small human being in a formal lavender dress. He'd only ever seen her in sweatpants or capris and a loose T-shirt.

He stared at her for a while, turned and went back to the hallway and waited for Willa. She came out in a minute and they walked to the parking lot together.

"Come stay with me and Luke," Willa said as they got into the car.

He hadn't seen her new house yet. They sat in the dark warmth of the car in silence. It was tempting to give her what she wanted. If he went with her, they would both pretend they'd never said terrible things to each other. He'd pretend he wasn't hurt, that he didn't need to wall himself off from her and their mother. He wanted to tell her about the lake man. He would sound crazy. The man swam through his head, turned like a goldfish around and around.

"I want to go home. I don't have the energy for Luke."

"What energy?" said Willa.

"I have to be the good brother."

"Luke doesn't expect anything from you. I only expect you to be civil, which doesn't have to be hard."

"I can't do it tonight," he said, a bit too loud.

"Why don't you talk to me?"

Willa started the car and pulled out of the funeral home lot. As they drove back over the bridge to Poughkeepsie, the bridge lights clicked on, white and blue on either side of the car. At the train station, he got out. "Thanks," he said. He didn't turn around.

S hivam climbed the stairs to Justin's apartment, alerting the dog in the apartment below. The air grew oppressive when he reached the third-floor landing. He hadn't seen Justin since they left the lake house two weeks ago. He'd gone home to visit his parents, had spent time with his friends, who complained he'd neglected them since meeting Justin.

Justin answered the door and allowed him in. The air in the apartment smelled old and Justin wouldn't look at his face. He wore ratty shorts and no shirt. The air conditioner wasn't running. The stink of Justin's armpits wafted into Shivam's face, and when Justin spoke, his breath prickled Shivam's nose hair. He'd been drinking. Shivam had seen this before with other guys: the day things changed. He'd worried about it at the lake house. If you rushed into being close, it scared people. He didn't think Justin would be one of those men, but this person bore little resemblance to Justin.

Shivam had encountered casual cruelty when he'd first started dating. Anytime he didn't date other South Asian men, he ran into racism. All flavors of it, from the baldly stated "I'm not attracted to Indian men" to more subtle strains, which appeared later, after a few dates. He would find himself in bed with someone and would begin to suspect that they were not interested in him as a person. It was hard to pinpoint why. Often just a feeling. Inevitably, these would be the men who admitted, without shame, that they were into him because he was Asian, that they'd always thought Asian men were beautiful, as if he'd be flattered.

He worried Justin might be one of these men, but he knew somehow that he wasn't. Maybe it was that Justin seemed so careful, so worried about being with him. At the wedding, Shivam debated whether people were staring at them because of their age difference or because of their race difference, but he didn't speak to Justin about it. They would have to talk about these things, eventually. He wanted to love Justin, and he did. He walked around in a drugged state, forgetting his previous life, even putting aside his worries.

Dirty dishes covered the counters and were piled on the coffee table. Liquor bottles stood empty on the floor by the couch. He must not have been going to work. He was an alcoholic and had hidden it really well before, somehow, or Shivam had not wanted to notice.

Justin returned to the couch, where he'd created a cradle of pillows.

"Did you not go to work?" Shivam said. He picked up two bottles and put them on the coffee table. "Do you have a drinking problem or something?"

"Come here," Justin said. He put out his hand and gestured. "Come here."

Shivam sat on the edge of the couch and allowed Justin to hold his hand.

"Why are you here?" Justin said.

"I'm here to see you, remember?"

"But why?"

"I don't know. Because."

"You were gone a long time," Justin said. "I forgot about you."

"You forgot about me?" Shivam said.

"I didn't. I didn't," Justin said.

"I don't like you this way," Shivam said. He took his hand out of Justin's. "I'm going to leave. Call me when you're not whatever you are right now."

Justin's body heaved slightly, as if he were trying to shrug. This reminded Shivam of a dream he had in which his mother was waiting in a room in their old house. In the dream she was facing away from him. He went to her and tapped her on the shoulder and she said, "Hello?" the way you'd say it to a stranger. Justin had turned onto his side. Shivam tried to make himself stand. I'm already gone.

Willa received a letter from Justin, which explained he needed time away from her, time away from thinking about the past, of which she reminded him. As if she could do anything about that. The handwriting worried her. A sentence would begin with clarity and run into trouble by the end, the words transforming into hieroglyphics. From what she could make out, Justin wanted to create a new life and identity. He'd let her back in if she took him for what he was now and let him forget his victimhood. Could she be the sister of his new life? he asked.

She put the letter in the trash. He sounded altered. Luke found it there, beside a heap of coffee and potato peels. "You must miss him," he said.

Luke and Justin had never liked each other much. Justin had issues with straight men. It took a lot of effort for him to trust them, and he'd never given Luke a chance. Luke, who was so easy and open. "Yes," she admitted. "I miss him. But maybe it's better if I leave him alone."

• •

Her dioramas now lived in boxes in a storage facility she paid for, though there was plenty of room for them at the new house. Luke didn't ask about it, had probably forgotten. She was glad. Luke would be too supportive and encouraging and it would make her feel guilty.

She'd abandoned them right after the wedding, deciding instead to simplify herself, to be a nurse and be happy with it. For a few weeks, she didn't think about the dioramas, and it didn't occur to her to pick up a pencil and sketch. If she lived fine without it, she wasn't meant to do it. Leave art to the people who must do it. One day, she sat at her mother's table, eating a bowl of spaghetti with butter and parmesan, a meal that had always comforted her.

"Are you doing your little models?" her mother asked, unprompted.

Willa couldn't think of another time her mother had asked about the miniatures, except when Willa was a kid and her mother wanted her to clean her room and organize her collection.

"It's good to have a hobby. I wish I'd developed one, now I have all this time."

It was the word *hobby* that troubled Willa. It more than troubled her. It enraged her. "I'm not doing it anymore," Willa said. "And it's not a hobby."

"Making models isn't a hobby?" Grace said. "That's exactly what it is. Nothing wrong with it. The ones I was allowed to see were cute."

"I didn't think you were interested," Willa said.

"I don't know how you learned to make those little people," Grace said. She had eaten before Willa arrived. It bothered Willa to eat while her mother watched with her hands folded.

Her mother had never seen the dioramas about Justin. Willa imagined Grace wouldn't recognize them for what they were anyway. She would see a doll house, toys. Maybe that's what they were.

In the car on the way home, the need to make something reappeared, and it was similar to a desire to show her mother she was an artist, a word she'd never used to describe herself. She wanted to start up again, but it would be harder now. Anytime she took a short break from sketching or sculpting, it was hard to pick up her sketchbook again, to sit at the desk and imagine building an environment. She knew she could do it, as she'd done it before, but it still felt impossible.

Her mood soured. She was short with Luke and her patients.

Before they got married, she and Luke had briefly lived together in his apartment. Now they tried to decide how to live their lives in a house together. She never filled the cavernous refrigerator. Boxes remained unpacked in the living room or open and spewing packing paper. She didn't want to decide where things would live.

Luke tried to help. They sat on the floor together, unwrapping items she'd saved from her old apartment, knickknacks she'd bought at the antique shops in New Paltz. In her old apartment, they'd felt special and valuable, but here she placed them on a shelf and they were revealed to be junk.

Luke unwrapped a glass whale she'd loved for years. He handed it to her and she brought it to the mantel, tried it there, took it and brought it to the bookcase. Was it the house or was it her? The whale didn't belong here. She left it on the bookcase for Luke's benefit, but when he went to bed, she grabbed it and rewrapped it in packing paper and put it back in the box. The next evening, they worked on unpacking another box.

"It's too messy in here," she said. "I can't concentrate."

"If we unpack more, we can get rid of some of the cardboard," Luke said. "You're not supposed to take three things out of a box and move on to another box. Let's finish one box and get rid of it."

Willa stared at the box she'd placed the glass whale inside. She pulled out a few objects from it and gave them to Luke to unwrap. All but the whale. Around midnight, when they were both tired, she waited for Luke to fall asleep. Then, she got up and dug through the box and found the whale, still wrapped in paper. She didn't unwrap it. She threw it in the garbage.

The hospital took over her life; she worked extra shifts, coming home after Luke had been asleep for hours. In the living room, she'd sit on the couch and watch the light outside bloom from velvet purple to peach, too exhausted to move to the bed. With nothing to distract her, she thought of Justin and Shivam, assuming Justin had somehow gotten what he wanted, had succeeded in acquiring his new life without her. Maybe she'd held him back all of these years without realizing it, when she assumed she was caring for him.

If he was doing better, if he was happy, she would stay away and try to let him go from her mind, concentrate on her life with Luke, who wanted her to show interest in the house, in making it her own. Justin and Shivam had moved to a nice apartment, she imagined, somehow able to afford it. Justin didn't think about Grace, or Nick, or Mrs. Flores, or anything that came before Shivam. When the sun had fully risen, she got off the couch and went to take a shower.

Once a week, she met Jenny for a night out, and tried not to let her exhaustion ruin their time together. Jenny possessed teenage energy. She didn't have a partner and didn't want one. Her days were spent with farmers, horse people, or alone, which she preferred.

One night in December, Willa drove out to the little house Jenny had moved into the year before. An old-growth forest surrounded the house. Out in the gravel driveway, Willa listened in the dark to the deep quiet, until it broke with the sound of a night bird.

They sat by the woodstove drinking vodka. Jenny brought out a giant bowl of greasy popcorn sprinkled with nutritional yeast, the kind they'd eaten at her house when they were kids. Willa licked her buttery fingers, her stomach sour.

Jenny handed her a wrapped package. Christmas was three weeks away. Inside the package were colored pencils and a sketch pad, the kind you'd buy someone who wanted to try drawing. "I thought it would be funny," Jenny said. "They're the cheapest ones."

"I love it, thanks. The paper's perfect." Willa slid the

pad into her bag along with the pencils. They would make their way into a drawer and she'd forget about them.

"I'm not pressuring you," Jenny said.

"I know," Willa said. "But I don't have anything to give you back. This was a sneak attack."

The room was oppressively warm. The air filled with Jenny's smell: natural detergent, Egyptian musk, her breath remembering the alcohol they'd drunk. Willa was happier here than at home with Luke, but it wasn't Luke's fault. For her, romantic love had always paled in comparison to her love for Jenny, which had the bulk of years behind it.

During a lull in the conversation, Jenny fell asleep on the floor by the woodstove. Willa moved to a chair and turned on a lamp on the side table. She pulled the pencils and drawing pad out of her bag and opened both. The pencils were garish and beautifully sharpened all in a row. She had not drawn anything in a year. Drawing had always come naturally to her. When she was making dioramas, she mostly drew plans rather than sketched from life. To engineer the world into fuzzy existence—to have brief control, if all went well. She huddled under the lamp next to the couch and turned a few pages into the pad. She couldn't start on the first page.

• •

Grace stayed in bed for days with a sudden illness. She had been working as a part-time clerk at the library in town, a filthy place, all those hands and old books, the filthy fingers of children. Men off the street with nowhere else to go during the day. And she touched the books, reshelved, helped elderly people with the computers.

A person touches their face often and never thinks about it. She tried to wash her hands as much as possible. She'd caught something. Her head weighed her down, and the muscles in her legs ached but wanted her to move. She tossed and turned in bed until the sheets stuck to her. The inside of her mouth tasted poisonous.

She had always been insensitive, she knew. Arthur had called her rough. When they fought, she knew how to hurt him. The fever took her under into sleep and she dreamed about him, alive again and standing in the room with her. Arthur leapt at the bed and tore her out of it, dragged her through the apartment into the bathroom, where he put her in the tub. It felt real, but it wasn't, and she knew this in the dream. Once in the tub, he removed her clothes and scrubbed her itchy skin. She awoke scratching her arms, which she noticed were now covered in a red rash.

On the second day, she rose and washed herself, the hot water burning her feet and raw hands. In the living room, with a blanket around herself, she called Willa, but the phone kept going to voicemail. She tried Luke and caught him.

"Grace? Is everything okay?"

"Yes. Fine. I can't get ahold of Willa. I was worried." She tried not to cough.

Before he hung up, Luke promised to let Willa know she was trying to reach her. The phone grew cold in her hand.

She went into the kitchen, hunched over, and found the little scrap of paper in her address book. She never imagined needing the phone number written there and had almost thrown the scrap away when she'd first found it. She'd found it a week after Willa's wedding, in the bottom of the fancy purse she'd brought to the reception.

• •

In the other room, Sue vacuumed, though Grace begged her not to. She didn't want to lie there while her son-in-law's mother cleaned her mess, but understood that Sue did what she wanted to do to help. Since the wedding, they'd spoken a few times, but only when Sue called. Grace had been too embarrassed by her behavior on the night of the wedding. Until today. Now she was too sick. Too afraid to be alone.

At one point, before Sue arrived, she'd sat on the couch hyperventilating, listening to the unpleasant sound of the air wheezing in and out of her throat.

"I don't think vacuuming will cure me," Grace said when Sue finished the living room and brought the vacuum into the bedroom, the cord in her hand.

"You'd be surprised."

"Thank you," Grace said. "I'm mortified. I was always a clean person. Obsessive about it. I'm sure my children would be happy to tell you. They always acted like it was abuse."

Sue squinted at the word *abuse*. "Better to grow up in a clean house," she said.

"I was always a clean person," Grace said again.

With Sue here, she noticed how she'd neglected her small space. It had happened so gradually. Leave a plate here. Tomorrow, I'll take it into the kitchen and clean it. Scrub the shower. Her arms didn't have the strength anymore. The mold became a little decoration in the corners of the tub. Why dust when there was no one around to be offended by it?

"I need you out of the bed now," Sue said. She didn't demand. There had to have been darkness inside this woman, but it had been smothered by light and would be hard to locate. It was easy to hate someone like that.

"Fine," Grace said.

"Do you need to lean on me?"

"No. I got up before." The effort to rise from bed and move to the cushioned chair in the living room took all of her breath.

"I think you have the flu," Sue said from the bedroom. Grace understood her bed was being stripped. She hadn't changed the sheets in a month. They were a layer of her skin.

When she was done changing the bed linens, Sue entered the living room and opened the windows.

"Oh, please don't," Grace begged her. "We'll freeze."

"Just for a little. You need the fresh air."

She brought Grace a glass of water and sat in the chair across from the couch. "Thank you," Grace said. "Willa would be mortified if she knew you were here. I'm an embarrassment."

"I'd say that's a plenty normal response for a daughter." Sue laughed. A nervous condition.

"She's busy," Grace said. "Taking care of sick people. I rate low on her list of priorities. Cancer cells, then me."

"When you're young, only your life matters to you. I'm sure she'll feel terrible when she gets your messages."

"She won't," Grace said. "She's not speaking to me. She's tired of being in the middle of me and Justin."

"Are you hungry?" Sue asked. She went to the kitchen without being invited to and opened the refrigerator. From the couch, Grace watched her move around the kitchen. In ten minutes, a plate of eggs sat in front of Grace.

"I said terrible things," Grace said as the eggs grew cold. "I don't know if I believed what I said. We've always had trouble. Maybe it's my fault. I just never understood him, and it was so frustrating. I never liked him. I never liked my own son."

Sue listened and said nothing. Why had she said any of it to this woman who could never relate? Luke didn't even live in the same universe as Justin.

"Maybe you're too sick to have this conversation," Sue said. "But today, when you were frightened, you called me."

"I'm sorry," Grace said. "Please don't feel you have to stay. I don't enjoy being pitied."

"Just saying what I think. I don't have any pity. I saw how sad you were the night of the wedding and said to myself: She's the saddest person I've met in a while."

She might as well have set Grace's hair on fire. Grace coughed for half a minute. "Aren't you a saint?" she managed. "Why don't you take your holy ass out of my apartment."

Sue got out of the chair, but didn't leave the apartment.

She closed the windows. She wore her hair short, in a style she must have thought was sophisticated but reminded Grace of a little girl whose mother has cut her hair. She wore jeans that puffed out at the waist.

"It's too cold!" Sue said, as if it hadn't been her idea to open the windows in the first place. She produced a deck of cards from her bag. "Do you like cards?" she said.

"I only know how to play rummy," Grace said.

"Perfect." Sue shuffled and dealt the cards. Sue would win. A woman who carries cards in her pocketbook knows what she's doing. She'd dealt Grace a terrible hand, and as the minutes passed, her luck remained shitty. She didn't pay attention to what Sue picked up or laid out. Her mind wasn't in the game, and Sue easily won.

"Let's play another," Sue said. "You have to watch the pile and see what I'm picking up."

"I think I'm too sick to play this game," Grace said.

"One more," Sue said. "Don't give up so easily."

Sue dealt the cards again and won again soon after, but Grace had managed to put together three of a kind and part of a sequence.

• •

Afterward, Sue washed her hands at the kitchen sink and turned around with them dripping. "Do you have anything other than paper towels?"

"No," Grace said "Nothing clean."

"Oh well," Sue said. "I'll be back tomorrow." She left with her wet hands before Grace argued or begged her not to come back. The apartment had been reordered and smelled of lemon.

Grace turned on the TV and watched two hours of cooking shows. Around nine thirty, someone knocked at the door. It would be Sue again, or possibly Willa on her way home from work. Whoever knocked couldn't wait for her to make it from the living room, so they knocked again, three quick knocks. Willa didn't knock like that. So impatient.

The front door didn't have a peephole. She stood and waited.

"Mom, it's Justin."

"I'm sick," she said. "I can't see you."

"Please open the door." His voice was sluggish.

"You sound drunk."

"I came to say goodbye," Justin said. "I'm going away. I'm moving away."

"Where are you moving?"

"Open the door," he said.

"I don't want to get you sick," she said.

"Open it a crack," Justin said.

Grace opened the door but kept the chain on. In the dim stairwell, Justin looked like a Polaroid developing. He moved his face close to the opening. The smell of him overpowered her, and she stepped back from the door. Maybe it wasn't him. Maybe it was someone who knew of him, someone who'd come to hurt her.

"I'm going away," he said again.

"You and your friend are moving somewhere?" Grace asked.

"My friend?" Justin said. "My friend the lake man. He's coming."

"The Indian boy," Grace said.

Justin kicked the door. "His name is Shivam."

"Do you want me to call him for you?" Grace said.

"Mom, let me in. Just for a minute."

Grace came closer to the door again to show him her face.

"Justin, I can't let you in. I'm afraid."

"I'm nothing to be afraid of," he said. "I'm afraid, too. I didn't mean to scare you. Please, Mom. I took a train all the way here, and I got on a bus, and walked from the bus, and I got lost walking around in this neighborhood. All the houses and trees look the same."

"Do you want me to call him? Shivam," Grace said.

"No," Justin said. "I don't know where he is." His voice struggled. "If you're not going to let me in, I guess I'll go now. Goodbye." He put his fingers through the opening and kept them there until she understood and touched them with her own.

"Go home," she told him. "Promise me."

"I will," he said.

After she shut the door, she went to the window to watch him walk away. It took a long time for him to appear, but he did, trying to walk strongly. He staggered down the drive-way and disappeared around the corner.

She hurried to the phone and, after a coughing fit, dialed Willa again. The phone rang and rang. She called Luke again, but he didn't answer this time. Would it have killed her to let Justin in? Something had told her not to and she'd trusted it. She would not allow herself to feel heartless. She walked through the living room to the front door, opened it, and went out, down the stairs and into the yard. The air was cold and dry and froze in her nostrils. In the house behind her, the kids were awake and fighting and laughing. Their parents yelled at them. "I'm going to kill you if you don't shut up," their mother said.

In June, Jenny and Willa drove north to hike in the Catskills, taking a route Jenny and her father had hiked many times during her childhood. Wildflowers were in bloom, the air hot and fragrant. She and Jenny wore boots with long pants, tape around the ankles, and before starting out, Jenny sprayed Willa with insect repellent. Jenny had suffered from Lyme disease several times.

Willa struggled on the steep trails. Jenny was endlessly patient with her, waiting for her to catch up when she lagged behind, while she snapped pictures of early summer flowers, or stopped next to the trail to pee, or tried to record the sounds of birds you only hear in the woods.

After the hike, they descended out of the mountains in Jenny's car, and forty minutes later stopped in a town named after the mountains. A quiet place with old buildings. Some had been renovated. Shops and restaurants opened, people appeared on the street. Willa didn't find the town charming or whatever it was supposed to be. The new facades meant that the people who had previously lived in the town had been forced to leave. She and Jenny went into a bar, sat at one of the rough-hewn wooden tables, and ordered burgers.

Willa felt old and out of shape. She let the fries on her plate go cold. The bar filled with people, and soon all the tables were occupied. The lights dimmed, and the volume of the music increased. Willa leaned over the table.

"If I needed to," Willa said, "could I come stay with you at the cabin?"

"Of course." Jenny waited through Willa's silence. "Is something wrong with you and Luke?"

They didn't talk about him usually because Jenny didn't ask. Marriages didn't interest her. "No. Not really," Willa said.

"You know you have me," Jenny said. "And my place. Whenever."

Now Jenny must think she and Luke were having problems, and they weren't really. They weren't having problems, but they weren't happy, passionate. They weren't having a good time, and it was too early on to have stopped. She wouldn't tell Jenny this. "Yeah, I don't need it," Willa said. "I'm just asking because it's nice to know you have backup."

"All right. I'm your backup. I'm cool with that."

"You're not just my backup," Willa said.

"Do you have sunstroke?" Jenny asked.

"It's the house, I think," Willa said. "I don't like it. There's this little room across from our bedroom. It's where a normal person would put a nursery. Luke keeps calling it the office. My office. He doesn't need one. But what do I do with an office?"

"How about a studio?"

"That makes me feel like I could start my little hobby again, and it's too depressing."

"Stop thinking about it so much," Jenny said. "Why does it have to be torture? You should do it if it makes you happy."

Willa cringed.

"What?" Jenny said. "I don't get it. It's too complicated or something?"

A man walked by the window of the bar. Willa noticed him because he hadn't flowed by the way other people did. Walking through a dream, which happened to lead him across her view. His hand pressed against the glass to steady himself and he disappeared, leaving behind a white smear. Willa got up from the table and walked out onto the sidewalk. The sky burnished the tops of the buildings and made people in the distance into shadows. She moved to get a better look at the man. She watched his back, walking much faster, almost charging. The way he walked frightened her. She would normally avoid a person like him.

"Are you angry?" Jenny said from behind her.

"No," Willa said. "I thought I saw Justin."

"Where do all these people come from?" Jenny said.

There was no breeze, and the air smelled of cigarette smoke and people, their hair and lotions and perfumes. Bits of conversation, annoying voices, distracted her. Jenny disappeared back into the bar. Willa walked away from it, but only a few feet. Jenny joined her a moment later, and they walked together.

"It was probably him," Jenny said. "Does he still live over in Hudson?"

"I don't know," Willa said. "He must, but I don't know for sure." She counted in her head, back to the previous summer. She hadn't seen him for a year.

By the end of the block, she knew it was Justin. He hadn't cut his hair or shaved. He wobbled, sickly and dangerous. People avoided him and laughed when they were out of his reach. She hurried around a small group of smokers. When Willa reached him, she couldn't bring herself to touch him.

"Hey," she said. The man turned around.

He didn't recognize her, or acted like he didn't, and for a minute she worried about her ability to know if someone was her brother or a man who resembled her brother. Justin's nose gave him away. His clothes were stiff and ripped in places. His beard hair gleamed in the sun. He wouldn't speak. If she heard his voice, she would know. Jenny's hand slid over her shoulder, and Justin suddenly hurried away. He left a sweet, oniony smell behind: the smell of fields. Willa followed.

"Maybe you should leave him alone," Jenny said, also following.

"What's he doing?" Willa said.

They were now away from the crowds and on a street lined with rickety but pretty houses, all with tiny front yards and modest gardens. The land sloped downward. Ahead of them, Justin stumbled over the uneven sidewalk. All this time, she'd pictured him living with Shivam. She assumed they'd moved in together. She hoped he'd gotten his new life, whatever that meant. She'd been angry at him occasionally, at the foolishness of wanting to cut ties with her. He'd been so strong the last time she saw him and in his letter, telling her he didn't need her. Before that, he'd needed her so much.

"Justin," Willa shouted, and heard the sadness and begging in her own voice, which surprised her.

Justin stopped and turned around.

They caught up to him. Jenny hung back, but Willa wished she would take charge. Jenny would know how to handle this. Nearby, a woman walking a golden retriever stopped to watch them. Willa caught her breath. Justin glared at her with impatience. He wanted to be away from her, and it knifed through her. Sometimes, in the past, she'd wanted to be away from him herself. Was this how it felt to him?

"I'm not going anywhere with you," Justin said.

"Where are you staying?" she said. "With Shivam?"

"None of your fucking business."

"Why didn't you call me?" she said.

"I told you I don't want you in my life." He didn't shout. His words were soft, almost shapeless. A year ago, she'd sat by the river with him and had hurt him.

"This is ridiculous," Jenny said. "Justin, you're coming with us."

He turned away from them and started walking again.

This time, Willa grabbed his arm without thinking.

"Leave me alone, you fucking cunt!"

She did. She left his arm alone, and even though she'd already let it go, he wrenched it back. He walked faster than before, heading off to wherever he lived. Maybe he didn't live anywhere. She hated to think of him sleeping in a park or in a shelter. Where was Shivam?

She turned around and saw Jenny waiting for her a few houses away. They walked back to the car without saying anything, but Jenny put her arm around her as she cried. Once they were on the New York State Thruway, Jenny touched Willa's knee and Willa smiled to show she was all right. She would think of what to do, or she would do nothing, she would forget him. He'd looked so horrible, so angry. The tears wouldn't stop coming.

"I should have forced him to come with us," Jenny said.

"You couldn't have," Willa said. "Nobody could." It occurred to her that she hadn't fully watched him walk away. She might never see him again and already she couldn't remember what that last moment had looked like, when he turned away.

Part Four

THE MINIATURES

Willa missed Justin's homecoming. She had been in school, floating through her day from class to class, without the knowledge that her brother was back. Her mother hadn't told her it was happening. Later, Grace said of course she'd told her, why wouldn't she?

After school, she walked in the front door and Justin was sitting in the living room. He used a cane in each hand to help him stay upright. His body looked skeletal and wild, like a boy raised by wolves. She wasn't prepared. She hadn't gone to see him during the months he was in the hospital because her mother thought it would be too hard for her to see him. Willa didn't try to imagine what he'd look like. She thought he'd look the same. But he didn't.

Their mother sat on the couch with her arms around him, his bristly head resting on her shoulder. His head had been closed with staples; where the staples had been removed, there was a large crescent scar. Ugly pink.

Justin's eyes fixed on the carpet. Grace cried. Willa put herself in the wingback chair, carefully, to watch her mother cry. Love cracked and gushed inside her to see her mother's tears. She didn't know if it was seeing her mother be weak and soft, or seeing her crying over Justin, hurt by what had happened to him, but Willa didn't want it to stop.

• •

The police came to speak to Justin. Willa was used to them being around. The last time they came, Grace brewed coffee and they sat at the table talking.

"Your father was one of the best," an overweight cop said to Justin, and Justin's eyes examined the dark uniform.

Willa waited for him to respond. He didn't. "Thanks," she said for him. Just in case.

Her mother asked her to leave, as if Willa couldn't handle the conversation. Had the officers not been there, she would have argued. Instead, she pretended she was going to her room, but she secreted herself in the linen closet in the hall, which shared a wall with the kitchen. Much of what she heard sounded melted. The spike of Nick's name drove through her ear now and again.

Later, she drifted into Justin's room. He kept the door closed all the time now. It made him feel safer, he said. Grace didn't argue with him about it. He sat on the bed with a deck of cards spread in front of him on the blanket. There was a railing on the edge of the bed so that he wouldn't fall out of it during the night.

"They said I wasn't there when the kid died," he whispered.

Did he not remember Matt's name? It was possible. Some of his past had been erased. She almost said: *Matt. The boy who died was named Matt.* People said the name to her all the time. "Matt," someone would say as they passed her in the hall or the cafeteria, as if it were an insult. They didn't have to say anything else.

"Who said you weren't there?"

"It was Nick," Justin said. "They told them, the uh, police, I wasn't there. They said I ran away. Nick did it."

Most likely, he remembered none of it and was telling her a story. He looked at her and tried to smile, but it gave her the creeps. He looked like an android pretending to be reassuring. She smiled back at him so he would stop.

He hadn't been there. Or the police couldn't prove he had been there. She didn't know. At school, the message reached her daily. *It's your brother's fault.* Matt had been popular, a baseball player.

"I was there. I didn't run away. I was hiding."

Willa came around to the foot of the bed and climbed onto it to be closer to him. "If they say you weren't there, you weren't there."

"I said Nick took me and I didn't want to go."

"He kidnapped you," Willa said.

He started crying. His tears copious. Drool leaked out of his mouth. He laughed occasionally for no reason, too. It would ring out in the middle of the house. She couldn't allow him to be this laughing and crying person. The cry was like something he was chasing, something that he'd tried to hold on to. Out of control. She slid away from him.

Grace appeared in the doorway, hurried through it, and grabbed her arm. "You're upsetting him."

Willa slipped off the end of the bed and let Grace take her out of the room. They both didn't go back.

• •

Grace drove Justin over to Poughkeepsie to something called Neuro-Recovery. Willa didn't go along, only imagined what went on there. He needed to go somewhere and learn things; he had to be rehabilitated.

"He's different," she told Jenny. They sat next to each other in their only class together. The first bell had not rung yet.

"Can I come over? I want to see him."

"You don't know him. You won't be able to tell."

"I just meant to visit. Not gawk at him."

"No," Willa said.

After school, they hitched a ride with Jenny's father. At the farm, she lay by the woodstove with the dog while Jenny read aloud from *A Tale of Two Cities*, until her father told her to stop. It was putting him to sleep. He turned on a movie, and they shared a bowl of greasy popcorn with nutritional yeast. Willa let the dog lick her hands until they were hot and soggy. When she called home, her mother answered.

Willa waited to be yelled at.

"Where are you?" her mother asked.

"Jenny's. I want to stay here. I'm sorry I didn't call earlier."

"I knew you were fine," her mother said.

• •

When Willa talked to him, it took time for her words to reach him. Something flicked on behind his eyes, and finally he answered her. Whatever she asked him annoyed him. They stood in the kitchen. She laid slices of cheese onto bread. "Do you want something to eat?"

He sat at the table with cards in front of him to help with his cognitive function. The card game was called Memory. It was the exact game they'd played as kids, with illustrations of different foods, household items, animals, or symbols on the cards. You put them down in a grid face up, flipped them over, and tried to remember where the matching cards were. He glanced at her and she watched it happen. That life appeared in his eyes as the information reached his brain.

"Yes," he said.

On Justin's birthday, Shivam threw him a party. It couldn't be a surprise because Justin didn't enjoy surprises, and he and Shivam had been trying to be kinder to each other, trying to respect what the other wanted. A small group of their close friends moved about the house, eating off paper plates. They lived on the lake full-time now, in a moderately nicer house than the one they'd rented in their younger years. Shivam taught online classes from home and drove twice a week to the community college in Troy, to teach in person. Justin worked part-time at a hotel in a little town nearby called Comet. It was a quiet town and had become a weekend spot for city people. Three times a week, he sat at the front desk, answered the phone, checked people in. Three times a week, he enjoyed telling people who asked him to take their bags to the elevator that this was not that kind of place.

In the living room, someone opened the top of the woodstove and put in a hunk of wood. The house filled with the dusty smell of fresh ash. Some of the other full-time lake dwellers stopped by, brought beer, stayed for a drink, and left.

Shivam was in the living room, laughing at something.

Their best friends, Tony and Aron, had brought the cake, which Tony now pulled from the refrigerator and uncovered. Tony had baked the cake and decorated it. Justin loved Tony, who he had held at a distance for a few months after meeting him, because he found it hard to trust his big, hulking masculinity.

Aron softened Tony. Aron was light on his feet and light of voice. He drank so much he was now the center of attention, trying to get Shivam to dance with him in the tight living room. Justin took the opportunity to drink a glass of champagne someone had left on the counter. Tony watched him do it, but Justin didn't care. He had been sober for four years. He remembered little of what it had been like to fail at living a normal life. Losing his job and apartment. Those things had happened, but the snapshots had been lost.

He remembered losing Shivam for a time, how much work it had taken to become well enough for Shivam to come back. Shivam hadn't disappeared completely, but he'd transformed into a supportive friend, which wasn't enough for Justin. He'd used that as motivation, the torture he felt when confronted by the distance between them.

The champagne burned his throat. He followed it with a glass of water with lemon, afraid Shivam would notice the champagne on his breath. In the week or two before the party, he and Shivam had fought about having liquor there at all. Justin recruited Aron and Tony to persuade Shivam. People would have more fun if they were drinking, and it wasn't as if Justin would get drunk while they all watched.

Tony turned from the cake, picked up the glass Justin

had drunk from, and put it in the sink. It struck Justin as funny that Tony would do this, as if he were trying to help hide the evidence. Justin touched Tony's ear and leaned in to kiss him on the mouth. Tony's silver-and-brown beard tickled Justin's upper lip. He had no reason to kiss Tony.

Justin looked into the living room at Shivam, who was watching them, and Aron, who laughed. Tony put his hand on the side of Justin's face.

"I just remembered something," Justin said.

"What?" Tony said. The kiss hadn't embarrassed him. Tony remained Tony. Smooth and upright, even-toned. He was the only person at the party wearing a dress shirt with the buttons done all the way to his neck.

"Do you remember when we first met you guys?" Justin said. "The night you'd all gotten drunk. I was the only one who hadn't. And we almost slept together. All four of us! I was stone sober and I knew exactly what I was doing."

Tony laughed. "I can't imagine thinking about fucking you now. Gross."

"Thanks," Justin said. He lived a dream-life here, one he would wake from with disappointment rather than relief. His life here was small. He drove from the lake to Comet, on a two-lane highway, and back again, never stopping anywhere that would intrude on the dream. Shivam would usually be home when he arrived, and they sat on the deck together, or Shivam went to the bedroom to read, and Justin swam or watched TV. Once or twice a week, they remembered to have sex. He felt close to losing Shivam all the time, though Shivam never gave him a reason to feel this way.

After the guests left, Tony and Aron stayed behind. Aron took his shirt off and hung it on the back of a kitchen chair and stood at the sink to do the dishes. He always took his shirt off to do the dishes. He didn't want his clothes to get spattered with soap and water.

"You kissed Tony," Shivam said. "Were you drinking?"

"No," Justin said. "I don't know why I did it."

"I'm not mad," Shivam said. He smiled. "I thought it was nice."

Aron came away from the sink with his wet hands.

"Close your eyes," Aron said to Shivam.

Shivam obeyed. If you didn't do what Aron wanted, he would torture you with begging. He put his face close to Shivam's.

"It's only fair," he said, and kissed Shivam, who laughed, ruining a good kiss. Justin grew aroused, though nothing would happen between the four of them tonight. They had moved on to something else, though it wasn't outside of the realm of possibility for them all. Those feelings were always in the air, and he loved these men so much, the thought of holding them, being naked with them, kissing them, didn't disturb him. It had been fun to kiss someone besides Shivam, but when he thought of opening their relationship, or finding someone else, he grew tired and sad. He didn't want to be with anyone else; he wouldn't find someone who loved him, contended with him, the way Shivam did.

"Thank you for my party," Justin said to Shivam.

Aron went back to the sink.

"I drank a glass of champagne," Justin said. "Only one."

"Okay," Shivam said.

"We can kiss each other," Tony shouted from the living room. "Our friendships are not like straight people's. They're better."

"I guess," Shivam said.

"We're lucky," Tony said.

"You won't be forced into it," Aron said, looking over his furry shoulder. "Not again, anyway."

After they'd gone, Shivam went to bed. Justin waited for a while, then stood in the doorway of the bedroom to listen to Shivam breathing. A sound he loved and hated, depending on the situation. When he was in the throes of insomnia, he would lie in bed and listen to Shivam's breathing, to the slow warmth of his sleep, and think about leaving forever.

He went into the bathroom to wash his face and let the water run until it turned hot, which took a long time.

• •

Justin stood out on the deck and looked into the dark over the water, which was somehow a heavier darkness during winter. The other side of the lake was invisible, as no one lived in those houses this time of year, no one to put on a light. You saw nothing, which was what was there. Nothing. Particles. Invisible somethings.

He turned and saw himself in the glass of the sliding doors, and the flickering living room beyond, with only the woodstove lighting it.

In the yard, his boots crunched on the thin layer of icy

snow. You only had to walk one two three four five six seven eight paces before you got to the water; there was a dip of the land that plopped you right in. The summer he and Shivam moved out here, they stayed up late, giddy, and took off their clothes in the yard and carefully slipped into the water. It was a different summer than when they'd first come here, a better summer.

While in the lake, which had been black and terrifying, Shivam asked him if he felt safe. *Don't you?* Justin asked. Shivam put his arms around Justin. The night quiet except for the chimes of tree frogs and katydids, and their own limbs moving the water. No, he hadn't felt safe at all. He should have. He felt happy, but it had been laced with something, as if a tiny creature in the water had entered his body. He remembered thinking exactly that, but not saying it aloud, swimming away from Shivam and out of the water onto the lawn, but after a minute Shivam joined him and he couldn't see Shivam touching him in the dark, couldn't see Shivam's mouth on his dick, only felt it, which overwhelmed him and made him gasp. He used his hands to find him. He licked skin, grabbed the ball of Shivam's bicep and found that with his mouth and kissed it. As Justin's eyes adjusted to the dark, he pulled Shivam on top of him. He remembered shivering with adrenaline. They would be new people to each other here.

Behind him, the motion sensor light on the deck snapped off. He stepped out, expecting to plunge into the freezing water, but his boot hit solid ice and he walked blindly out a few feet before stopping. Somewhere ahead of him footsteps smeared against the ice. Someone walked toward him. Nothing to be afraid of here. This was his home.

Clouds scabbed the sky, so the stars were not visible. The steps likely belonged to an animal, a deer maybe. Shivam would say it was a deer, but that wasn't the answer. The answer wasn't available. He'd always been fine with not knowing the answer to every question, though most people wanted explanations. Sometimes, he was certain Nick had died and was haunting him all these years, and haunting meant you experienced a kind of crookedness nearby or inside. Nick may have been alive in jail, or out of it.

Once, he'd seen Nick's face on a TV show about wanted criminals. Nick's young face with a computer composite of what he might look like now. At first, he thought he was imagining it. His skin turned cold. Sweat broke out all over his back. He stood up from the couch and watched from inches away, not breathing until the faces left the screen. His ears closed up and he couldn't hear what the host was saying about Nick.

He called Willa. Why was Nick in his TV? Why should he be confronted with that face again without warning? She didn't answer the phone. He couldn't remember what he'd done that night to rid himself of that face.

It had been years since he'd heard any updates about the investigation. In his teens and twenties, he'd called to inquire about the investigation once a month, then twice a year, then ceased to call. He always imagined Nick would end up in jail, but he'd disappeared, the way some people were able to do. Did he rid himself of the car? Was he living in Mexico, sunburnt, afraid to involve himself with anyone? Had he drowned in the ocean? Had he killed himself, unable to live as a fugitive?

Justin doubted it. Willa eventually suggested they try to forget about Nick completely. She could do that, maybe, but how could Justin? No one knew, not even Shivam, that Nick entered his mind every day of his life.

For a long time, Justin's anger focused on the police, who couldn't find the person everyone knew had killed that boy and had tried to kill Justin. Of course, they had tried to find him. Nick had been seen in Arizona, but not captured. Now and then, over the years, someone would call in a tip, but Justin knew it wouldn't be Nick, or if it was, Nick would slip away.

He'd once thought Nick lived nearby him in Albany. It chilled him and embarrassed him to think about it. He'd been so afraid, and it hadn't been Nick at all.

The footsteps grew louder. The closer they got, the less real they became, until Justin was certain he'd invented them. A bad feeling overcame him. He'd lost sense of which direction he should have been heading. Lately, he couldn't be sure of what was real and what wasn't. He turned to the dim light inside the cabin, the glowing woodstove. He went in that direction, moving faster than he should have over the ice.

Back inside, he closed and locked the sliding doors. A sound came from the center of the house. It wasn't a human sound. Not Shivam. Something musical and familiar. He walked onto the linoleum floor outside the bathroom, and his boots slapped water. He expected a dripping man to be waiting there, but it was the sink, the faucet running from when he'd turned it on earlier, overflowing.

For a long time, Justin pretended to be dead, pretended for an audience inside him, for Willa and his mother, his classmates, and especially Nick. Justin didn't know how much time had passed since Nick had left him on the forest floor, but he worried he would fall into death if he went on pretending. His body felt wet and cold. When he breathed, pain galloped through his head and lungs, up his throat and to the left and right, to both shoulders. Insects crawled over him. He imagined beetles but didn't see them. The sun had disappeared. The insects came to see if it was their time. When he could move again, he would somehow find himself back home. He would get there and be alive.

A light appeared, and the trees broke it apart. A familiar sound followed it, like wind with debris inside it. Nick's car at the curb across the street from school. Nick's car. A door slammed, and Justin shut his eyes. He wanted to run, but his body had grown accustomed to death. He looked in the only direction he could, through the trees, toward the place where the light had come from, and a figure approached, hurrying, and it was Nick.

For a few minutes, Nick stood over him. Justin kept

his eyes closed, but felt Nick, heard him breathing, saying something to himself in a low voice. Nick's foot nudged him, shook him.

Go away, go away, I'm dead. I'm not here anymore.

"Justin?"

He tried not to breathe. The breath inside his chest a little ball of blue light. He pictured it hiding itself behind one of his lungs, lighting it up.

Cold soft dirt, crackling leaves, needles, stones, all of it caressed his arms and face. The sound of Nick working, cursing. He covered Justin with the forest floor, the smell of blackened leaves. Nick cried and sucked snot back into his nose. Justin had never seen him cry, and he knew Nick was crying for himself, not for what he'd done.

Shoes crunched on the earth and took Nick away. Justin opened his eyes and saw black. He took in as much air as he could, and pine needles and dirt fell into his mouth. The dirt entered his ears and nose; it muffled the pain in his head and put out his lights. Nick got into his car and Justin followed him with his mind. Nick didn't turn on the radio. He drove in silence, turning the heat up to rid his body of the damp cold from the forest floor. He didn't look at the rearview or side mirrors.

He wasn't Nick at all anymore. He was a man driving somewhere, moving quickly, and he would have to be a new man right away, in new clothes and a new car. This wouldn't kill him. He would be fast and relentless. Who knew where he was going? Behind him, the memory of a boy whose name already faded.

In her new diorama, Willa placed a figure on a freestanding stage covered in false grass. A young man, but not Justin. He never appeared in her work anymore. She used her dreams and the stories Luke had told her, and warped them. This young man she placed on the grass, stationed behind a cow. His arm reached inside the animal. A funny thing to do, to move the arm gently so that it entered the hole she'd made in the cow's rear end, as if it would hurt the cow.

Several more cows stood by with other young men behind them, some with their bodies halfway inside the cows. She'd been working all year on a series of these dioramas. One of them, which showed a line of cows witnessing a wedding, was in a group show in a gallery in Hudson.

Today, after she'd finished with the last cow diorama, she spent a few hours painting men, peering through a magnifier, until her eyes burned and hurt when she blinked. The men were for a new project; they would be placed in a room together. She wanted a group of people in a space, without explanation or a focus. She'd drawn a plan out this time, and it filled her with anticipation and dread and hoped it would do so to whoever would end up seeing it.

When she finished painting the men for the day, she arranged the completed dioramas on a long table by the window, so the mid-morning sunlight cast over them. She sat at the table and placed the camera on the surface to keep it steady. Outside, the leaves on the trees were new and pale green. She lived on the first floor of an old house, not far from the house she'd lived in years ago, Mrs. Flores's house. Just outside and to the left of her front door she'd dug a square of dirt where she'd planted tulips in the fall. Some had come up and bloomed, and some had been eaten by the deer.

Luke had suggested she start posting her work online. She'd seen him at the "animal people" bar when she was out with Jenny. She still spoke to Luke, guilty because she'd ended it with him. How could he have been so happy with her when she'd been so obviously unhappy? She'd stayed with him longer than she'd wanted to. If only he'd been a bastard, but he was never anything but sweet, a little dull, sometimes withdrawn.

That night, enclosed in the dim bar with Jenny next to her, she felt brave. Luke's new girlfriend wasn't there, which helped. They spoke for five or ten minutes. He asked about work, about the dioramas, his hair completely gone now except for a ghost of it on the sides of his head where he'd shaved.

"I'm glad," he said, when she told him she was working on them again. "You should post pictures of them. I see people doing that."

"Yeah, I don't know," she said. She didn't use Facebook or Instagram or anything else.

Once she finished taking the photos, she loaded them onto her laptop and they appeared on the screen. The mid-morning sun did make it look like the people and events were in some version of real life. The sun warm and cream-colored, falling over the cows and men. What a brightly painted world.

• •

Whenever she'd worked for a long time, she recovered in front of the TV. Her mother, too, spent hours in front of the TV. Willa had quit trying to get her mother to exercise. Grace wanted to rot in her chair. Two hours into her stupor, the phone rang.

"Is this Willa?"

"Who's talking, please?" she said.

"I'm sorry, it's Shivam Mukherjee. I tried your old number, talked to Luke, and he gave me this number. I hope you don't mind."

"Of course not," she said. "It's nice to hear your voice." Her body started to shake. She got off the couch and paced with her phone.

"Justin's okay," Shivam said.

"Thank you," she said. "I wanted to ask but was afraid what the answer might be."

"He's okay, and not okay. I don't know what I'm doing," Shivam said. "How are you?"

She hadn't spoken to Shivam or Justin in four or five years. She'd lost track. He didn't come to mind during the day when she was at the hospital, and not when she worked on her new miniatures. He arrived when she slipped under the covers and the silence in the apartment poured into the bedroom. She'd started using a white noise app on her phone. Her body temperature rose and she tossed and turned, trying to get comfortable. The first year went by quickly, carried by her righteous indignation. He was a drunk and a screwup. He didn't want to live a good life. He'd rejected her offer of help, had called her a cunt. As the years passed, she thought she would have to be the one to break the habit of not being in his life, but she never did.

"Shivam, does he know you're calling me?"

"No," he said. He laughed a little. "He doesn't know how worried I am. I'm afraid to make him angry by being worried. He doesn't like me to remind him that he needs me, but he does. More than just me. He needs so much, but I'm supposed to act like he doesn't."

"I know," Willa said.

"He's forgetting things," Shivam said.

"He always forgot things."

"It's getting worse. It started with little things. Leaving the water running, the door unlocked. Going to the store and coming back with nothing. Now he forgets what we've already talked about."

She breathed into the phone and carried it into the workroom. The sun had passed over the house and the room had grown dim. She sat at her desk and put her hand under the magnifier. I wonder if he remembers me, if he remembers how long it's been.

"Maybe you should come here," Shivam said. "I was thinking. It might be good."

"Do you?" she said. "What would be good about it?" She examined the soft, magnified slopes of her palm.

"If you come here, you could help me get him to a doctor. He might listen to you."

"Have you asked him to go?"

"No," Shivam said.

"Jesus," she said.

Shivam cleared his throat. "We've been happy," he said. "In a routine for a long time. It's hard to ruin it."

"I don't know what to say," she said. "I don't understand."

"I guess you don't," he said. "It feels like our life is starting to end."

"It's not," Willa said. "I promise."

"You're the only person I imagined calling. I want you to tell me what to do."

Leave, she almost said. *Why do you stay?* He was a young man. He could get away. She couldn't have taken care of Justin for so long. They stayed on the phone with each other, not speaking much, until she lost her nerve and told him she would come.

● ●

It took her an hour, rummaging through the drawers in her workroom. She really was a pack rat, though she'd always denied it. She'd moved crates of old work from Mrs. Flores's to her house with Luke to here.

They weren't in the workroom. She went to the hall closet and pulled out a hard-plastic storage box filled with heavy things, took the lid off, and searched through. Inside, she found a fishing tackle box she hadn't looked in for years. A small version of Justin lay among other discarded bits and pieces, sculpted out of oven-baked polymer clay. His legs, painted like black jeans, had fallen off. She should never have made it or any other version of him.

• •

After Willa finished packing her bag, she left the house, locked the front door, put the bag in the trunk of her car, and sat in the driver's seat. She didn't want to go back into the house for any reason. Get out. Don't think about it too much. She hadn't told anyone. Not Luke—why would she? Not Jenny, who would ask questions, would offer to go along.

She drove out of New Paltz slowly, with the traffic heading away from the campgrounds, taking Main Street to the thruway. Somewhere ten miles north, she awoke, realized she'd driven all this way without thinking about it. She tried to remember passing familiar exits. At a rest area, she parked the car and took out her phone to scroll through her contacts. She should call someone, ask them to tell her what to do, but she didn't choose a number and didn't call anyone.

For years, she'd thought of herself as Justin's caretaker. Even during the times they didn't see each other. He lived in her mind, and she cared for him there. She experienced the fatigue of the caretaker, as if she'd really done it—grown fed up with him, gone on with her life. Maybe she'd only tolerated him.

No. She turned on the engine. Her only choice was to get back on the highway going north, but after seven miles, she took an exit and drove through an unfamiliar town until she found the entrance for the highway going south.

She didn't feel pain or shame or anything else until she reentered New Paltz. She had decided to go home. People crowded the sidewalks of Main Street on this beautiful afternoon. There were probably bands getting ready to play in a few of the bars. If she wanted to, she could go and sit and listen and not think. Shivam would hate her, would never try again, because she'd said she would come, but she would not come. In the driveway, she turned off the car and sat, listened to it relax and cool off. She would go into the house, and at first it would be unbearable and quiet, and she would feel awful. She'd turn the TV on, or the radio, or she'd stand in the shower until the feeling passed.

The sky cleared, and Tony and Aron appeared at Justin's front door on a Tuesday afternoon in May, without calling first, and suggested they take the boat out for the first ride of the season. Shivam had already gone, off to the community college to teach his one in-person class. The three sat on the deck watching the clouds dissipate. For an hour, they did nothing but this, and Justin read something in the silence between them. They didn't expect to be entertained by him. They were here to watch him, not just be with him. Now he was their responsibility, too, in a way he hated, but it was hard to be mad at them, or at Shivam. They didn't act like he was a burden, never intentionally.

Winter had lingered through March. Justin's eyes stung in the sun, as if he'd spent the entire winter in the cabin, never venturing out. They walked to the boat launch near Tony and Aron's house, and Aron helped Justin into the boat first. It was a medium-sized motorboat with two cushioned benches and enough room to move around. Aron sat behind the wheel wearing dark sunglasses and a backward baseball cap. He looked like a fugitive.

Recently, Justin had lost Shivam's trust. Two weeks

before, he'd put a frozen pizza in the oven and forgotten about it until the smell reached him in the living room. When the smell reached him so did the smoke. He panicked. How had the fire started? Where were the flames? In his mind he saw himself placing a frozen pizza on a baking sheet and sliding it into the oven. He opened the door to the cabin to let the smoke out, turned the oven off, and opened it. More dark smoke poured into the kitchen. He went around and opened the windows and the sliding doors. When he removed the pizza, it resembled something from deep space, an object that had traveled through the atmosphere.

Tony clomped onto the boat and removed the rope from the piling. They drifted until Aron started the engine and took them to the center of the lake. White foam trailed behind the boat, lingered, and disappeared. The late afternoon sun warmed Justin's neck and he removed his jacket and folded it onto his lap. Not all the trees around the lake were in full bloom; some were still struggling to come alive. The air smelled of blossoms.

"This is a perfect day," Tony said. "Isn't it?"

"It's nice," Justin said.

He wanted to ask them if Shivam had recruited them today. Last Tuesday, he'd been left alone, and Shivam had called to check on him when he reached the school. Did Shivam think he would be doing something wrong, that he might lose control somehow and destroy the cabin? He'd spent most of the evening on the deck, until the mosquitoes forced him inside. He didn't cook for himself. He watched TV until Shivam got home.

He'd never gotten used to the idea of friends wanting to be with him, not requiring anything in return. He feared they would leave him on a whim or he'd unintentionally offend them or try their patience and they would be gone. Shivam often assured him that Tony and Aron loved him. They would not suddenly change their minds about him. They had other friends around the lake, but none he and Shivam were as close to, none they spent so much time with.

Aron took the boat to the end of the lake where the big houses stood, some modern and crisp, with huge windows, others designed to look rustic and weathered, like they'd been there all along. Most of these houses were dark until June. Willow branches cascaded over the water at the shore. Aron cut the engine and they drifted in the quiet. The boat rocked, but not enough to make him sick. Hardly anyone else was out on the lake. There were times he couldn't bear to be on the boat. Once, they'd had to cut their outing short and bring him back to shore, where he'd collapsed in the grass until the world stopped twirling around him.

"Did you take the whole day off?" Justin said.

"Part of the day," Tony said. "It's too nice to be stuck in an office. I'm glad you weren't at the hotel today."

"I don't have that job anymore," Justin said. "They fired me. I thought you knew."

"No," Tony said.

"Shivam didn't tell you?"

"No, he didn't," Aron said.

Aron started the engine and took the boat past the first place he and Shivam had rented years ago. On the left was

Christmas Tree Island. The weeds grew large, some flowering. Water lapped onto the dirt.

"We should have a fire there sometime," Tony said. "That's what the cool kids do."

"I don't want to have a fire there," Justin said.

He heard the petulance in his own voice.

"Someone's a little grouchy today," Aron said.

"Well, someone doesn't like being babysat."

"Who's babysitting?" Tony said.

"Did Shivam ask you to take care of me today?" Justin said. "Be honest with me."

"He mentioned you'd be alone," Aron told him. He took off his sunglasses and moved the boat slowly forward.

Some of the year-round kids were in their yards or sitting with their feet in the water. Ahead of the boat, a boy failed to swim, going under and bobbing back up, while his sister stood on the shore yelling at him. Justin didn't recognize either of them. They were eleven or twelve. The boy in the lake wasn't thrashing, but he pawed at the water, drowning. Once, Justin had seen Shivam struggling, trying to swim back from Christmas Tree Island, a long time ago.

The boy's eyes rolled in his head and he ate the water.

Justin looked away.

Tony jumped in without saying a word. His splash clattered against the inside of the boat and soaked Justin. Aron hurried to the bow. Tony quickly retrieved the boy, who didn't fight him, and Aron reached over to help them. Tony pulled himself aboard again, panting. The boy fell into the boat with Aron holding his arms.

On the shore, the girl laughed, covering her mouth with both hands. Justin wished he had been the one to jump into the water and save the boy. At one time, he might have been strong enough, but he didn't trust himself anymore; if he jumped in the water, he might stay there, sink to the bottom. Tony sat the boy next to Justin, where he shivered, the cold radiating off him, his hair a black cap on top of his head. Justin touched the boy's clammy shoulder.

"Was that real?" Justin said.

The boy turned his head to the shore, where his sister had stopped laughing and now ran into the house. Had she pushed him or was this all a trick? Aron steered the boat to the dock and the boy came alive and jumped off and ran after his sister.

"You're welcome," Tony called after him.

· ·

While Tony showered, Aron cooked them dinner in their beautiful kitchen. Silver pots hung from a rack over the butcher-block island. Jars of beans and bottles of oil and vinegar were lined up on the counter. Aron improvised and created a mess. Justin had witnessed this before, but it had never become charming to him. Aron took his shirt off to cook, too. He breaded filets of fish, spilling breadcrumbs on the floor. When he turned around to talk, Justin saw breadcrumbs caught in his significant chest hair.

Justin couldn't get the little girl laughing on the shore out of his head. He wished he'd been able to coax information out of the boy before he'd run off. In another life, he'd had a little sister. He didn't think of that sister as the one he no longer spoke to. That brother and sister were long gone and easier to remember without guilt. He tried to think of a time when she'd been mean to him, had giggled the way the girl on the shore had giggled to see her brother in danger, but a memory like that didn't come, maybe didn't exist. Willa must have teased him occasionally. He'd been thinking about the little girl. Now he felt someone had left the room. Aron stood at the counter, busy. Oil popped in the pan. Who was missing? He expected to find the soaking-wet boy in the chair next to him.

"Do you think the little girl pushed her brother into the lake?" Justin said.

"I hope not," Aron said. "Shit."

"The little boy's fine, right?"

"Yes," Aron said. "He was okay."

"She was laughing," Justin said.

"She was? I guess I didn't notice. I saw Tony jump off the boat."

"You didn't notice her laughing? She was laughing hysterically."

"I believe you," Aron said.

Part of him wanted to leave, to go home and be alone until Shivam got back. Behind him, a cool breeze flowed through the open window, cooling the kitchen. Time passed slowly for him now that he had nowhere to be. The clock read 5:30 p.m. Somewhere his sister ate, watched someone cook, did whatever she did now. Kissed someone. Or sat alone. Painted with a tiny brush. He dreamed a small vivid dream about little trees and people, each tiny item came into focus before his eyes, and Willa made things with her hands and showed them to him. Little versions of himself he hated, resented, they sprang to life from Willa's hands and rushed at him, some of them carrying knives, all of their eyes painted and dead. Shivam walked in the door wearing his comfortable clothes, sweatpants and a T-shirt, sandals on his long feet. He sat beside Justin at the table. The kitchen smelled of fish. Justin rushed to put his hand on top of Shivam's hand—to steady himself, to remind himself he lived in the big world.

One day, after Justin came home from the hospital, a letter came in the mail, intercepted by her mother. Willa watched her turn the envelope in her hand. The address did not have a house number, only the street name. *Mrs. Dunham. Crane Street, Locust, NY.*

Justin moved slowly into the kitchen, away from the TV, which he was not supposed to be watching too much of. He used one cane now instead of two, and the rubber squeaked on the floor.

"What's that?" Willa asked. They did not get letters. Bills, sure, but not letters.

"Hold on," her mother said.

She unfolded the paper, read the first few lines, refolded it, and put it back into the envelope.

"What, Mom?" Justin said.

"Willa, take your brother out of the room."

"Take him where?"

Justin sat at the table. "Can I see?"

Willa understood. She put her hand on the back of his chair. She didn't touch him. He sweated through his clothes from the effort of moving around. He smelled. She didn't feel like a good person anymore. Not a caring person. *You just have to get used to him*, Jenny had told her.

"Is it mine?" Justin said. "Give it to me."

"You don't want it," Willa said. She spoke gently, trying to be offhand.

"Can I please see it?" Justin said.

"It's my letter," Grace said. "It's not for you." She took it with her to her bedroom and closed the door.

• •

Before Justin came back, Willa tried to think of something nice to do for him, so she went to the bookstore one day after school with Jenny and bought him a couple of the doorstop fantasy novels he loved. She kept them, two paper bricks, on the coffee table, so he'd see them right away.

"He won't need those," her mother said.

Now he held one of the books in his lap. He opened it and tried to read a sentence. It frustrated her to watch him, but Justin didn't seem bothered that he couldn't focus. Maybe he wanted to feel them in his hands and the rest didn't matter.

One Saturday morning, Willa came out of her room at nine and found him in the living room watching TV. His eyes were blue circled, his skin gray. He didn't sleep much. If their mother had been home, she would have switched the TV off and snapped at Willa for allowing it. It was the worst thing for him. He should be doing the work they'd given him at the Neuro-Recovery Center. They should go for a walk, try to get him stronger. He needed to be pushed, and he didn't complain when it was Willa doing the pushing. She forgot they shouldn't be lazy together anymore.

Justin struggled from his chair and went into their mother's bedroom. Willa followed.

"I bet she got rid of it," Willa said. He hadn't forgotten about the letter like she'd hoped.

Her voice struck him in the back and bounced. He continued searching with no regard for their mother's privacy, taking revenge on her for the years she had done the same. Willa had come home a few times herself to find her room changed in a way she couldn't pinpoint. With Justin, their mother didn't even try to hide. She once dumped his backpack out on the kitchen table in front of him when she suspected he was on drugs. Neither of them had ever invaded Grace's privacy. It hadn't occurred to Willa before that her mother owned private things. As Justin emptied the drawers, Willa cringed, afraid of what he might pull out.

Justin let a drawer fall off its track and onto the floor. He held the letter in his hand and stared at the envelope. Why hadn't his mother sent it to the police? Maybe it would help them find Nick? But no, she'd stuck it in her bedside drawer like it was something special.

He freed the sheet of paper from the envelope. His white T-shirt clung to his sweaty skin and turned translucent.

He held the letter slightly away from her and glared at her.

"I'm not going to take it from you," she said.

He shook and couldn't hold the page still to read it.

"What does he say about me?" he said, and handed it to her.

She sat on her mother's soft bed, which smelled so intensely of Grace's soap and perfume that Willa wanted to puke. She wanted to lie and say the letter explained something to Justin. Gave him something he needed. But what did he need?

The letter said:

If your looking for your son, he is in the woods on route 17 between Carver and Waterville in Iowa. About 2 mls w from Carver.

I'm sorry.

It was not signed. The writer had drawn a map of a road with arrows pointing into white space, which she guessed represented the woods where her brother's body should be waiting for someone to find him. Why would he send this letter? Out of guilt, cruelty? Stupidity? He would be caught. Someone who sent that kind of letter would be caught.

"It doesn't say anything," Willa said.

He yanked it out of her hand, ripping the corner, and read the first line aloud. He read better than she thought he would, though he halted a few times to go back and reread from the beginning.

"We should put it back," Willa said.

Justin folded the paper, but instead of putting it back in the envelope, he took it with him. Willa stayed in her mother's room, which smelled of the darkness of her mother, with a heavy curtain in front of the window. A single perfume bottle on the dresser. The perfume was called Happy. A relief to be alone, away from Justin. Whatever he did with the note, she didn't care. It was his life.

Later, their mother came looking for it. She hadn't changed out of her work clothes: creamy dress slacks and a soft blouse, strawberry colored. Willa hadn't bothered to clean up the mess in the bedroom.

"Where is it?" she asked Willa.

Willa pointed in the direction of Justin's room. She'd been sitting in front of the TV for hours and it had weakened her resolve. She shouldn't have pointed. He wouldn't trust her now. Willa followed her mother to Justin's bedroom.

"What did you expect?" Willa said. "You should have let him see it."

Grace ignored her. Justin's door was closed, but Grace had taken the doorknob off the week Justin came home, so she pushed it open and revealed him sitting on the bed. A pointy smell hit Willa from the other side of the room. Under the window, a black smear on the wall rose from the carpet to the windowsill in the shape of an urn. He had burned the letter there. Willa had not smelled smoke while she sat in the living room, and it frightened her. Her mother glared at her first. Justin couldn't keep himself from doing this, but Willa should have known. Why should she have guessed what he would do? Nothing made sense to her. She couldn't think straight in this house anymore.

• •

The previous summer, she and Jenny had gone to the nearby bird sanctuary and had found a cave out of which cold air seeped and caressed their faces and bare legs. They welcomed the cold, as the day had been scorching, but it had also unsettled her. The way it clouded out of the flat darkness of the entrance, which was large enough to duck into if they wanted to do such a thing. The hidden place terrified her. Water moved somewhere. She sensed living things inside. It was a place they went back to again and again. One evening, they stood by it and witnessed bats leaving for the night, and they crouched to get out of their way. Willa suspected Jenny hoped to build enough courage to go inside someday, but Willa wouldn't get there herself. Never.

One day, a cave opened inside Justin. Cold billowed out of him. Out of him and in their mother's direction. He would take nothing from her. He rejected his pills if they were offered by her hand. She gave them to Willa to deliver, but he didn't trust them.

"You planned this," he said to their mother. "To get rid of me."

"Of course I didn't," Grace said. "Why would I want to hurt you?"

To Willa it sounded like a lie, though it was true.

"You're a witch," he said.

Grace took him to his neurologist. Willa went along to keep him calm and let him know nothing evil would befall him. She didn't know what went on between the doctor, Grace, and Justin. She sat in the waiting room reading *Better Homes and Gardens*. Were there really people who decorated their homes seasonally? New pillows for fall. Different colored throws for spring, for winter.

• •

He suffered nightmares. She had them, too. Hers were about people invading the house. Kids from school. They broke in and stole things, and she panicked around the house, a trapped bird, trying to discover what had been taken.

She heard him walking around. Nails popped in the wood. He turned all the lights on. Grace got out of bed and tried to reason with him, but he couldn't be persuaded to become reasonable. He didn't sleep or go to school or remember things. His anger wouldn't cease, and it inconvenienced them more than anything. Who was he angry with? Nick? Their mother? Her? The anger shot out in every direction like a Roman candle on a spinning wheel. It pierced her and poisoned her with an anger she kept to herself. It distracted her. The books she was meant to read for school languished in her backpack. Math seemed frivolous. One day, she'd be able to leave them. She would move in with Jenny and would decide if and when she saw her family. It was wrong to blame Justin, but she blamed him.

One night, Grace pleaded with him. *Please*, she begged, *please go to your bed and be quiet. I can't live this way anymore. I need peace.*

No. No no no no, he shouted.

Willa heard a loud bang on the other side of her wall that shook her awake like a person. She turned the lamp on next to her bed and waited for her eyes to stop smarting. Half asleep, she put on the jeans she'd taken off before bed. Grace always turned the heat down at night, and the room was freezing. Her room now appeared childish to her, as if she'd woken up much older. Tomorrow, she'd take down the Madonna poster on the far wall, she'd put away the miniature trees on the dresser and the children's books in the bookcase. So many of these objects had been left out for years, and she'd stopped seeing them. The room wasn't a collection of choices. She'd put things in their place years ago and hadn't touched many of them since. It wasn't like Jenny's room, which reflected what Jenny was into right now. Willa got out of bed. She wanted to burn the lavender carpet under her feet.

She opened the door and went into the hallway. A glass fell onto the beige carpet and rolled to her feet. A few feet away, Justin lay on the floor, holding his hand against his chest. He'd stripped off his T-shirt and wore only pajama bottoms. Red blotches appeared all over his pale back. Grace retreated to her bedroom in her nightgown. Drawers opened and closed, and her closet door squealed. The bright light of the hallway invaded Willa. At night, the lights in the house glowed horribly white. Justin's hair gleamed black with sweat. What should she do, cover him? Leave him alone?

He had left a small dent in the wall with his fist. He cried, his face purple, like a little boy she'd seen once at the grocery store throwing a tantrum. One of his hands swelled. It couldn't be ignored, but she wanted to ignore it and go back into her bedroom and leave him on the floor. She turned and closed her door, so she wouldn't be tempted to go through it and lock herself inside.

Willa settled on the floor by him and watched him, but he didn't notice her there. She would stay. *Give me your hand*, she said, and he twitched at the sound of her voice and gave it to her, crying out in pain when she received it. He was small. Not her brother, but a little animal. He moaned, and his nose leaked. She held the warm hand as it swelled.

"You're going to be okay," she said. "I'm here."

Acknowledgments

This book would not exist without the dedication of my wonderful agent, Christopher Schelling, who supported and encouraged me during its writing, and would not let me give up on it later, and Leigh Newman, my brilliant editor, who brought me into the Catapult family. I'm so lucky to know both of you. Thank you to Alicia Kroell, Wah-Ming Chang, Nicole Caputo, Megan Fishmann, Rachel Fershleiser, and everyone at Catapult. It takes so many people to make a book, and I'm lucky to have worked with all of you to get here. Thank you to Sara Wood for a dream cover.

I must send special thanks to the people who read earlier versions of this novel. Thank you to Rachel B. Glaser for her keen eye and impeccable taste and vision; to Matt Katz, my best friend and a brilliant reader and human being; to Brett Welch for your invaluable suggestions. Thank you, Dan Fishback, for loving this book.

This novel was greatly improved by the involvement of

Joy Williams, who offered her time and gave crucial suggestions before the novel was submitted to my agent. I will be forever grateful. Thank you to Dan Chaon, Madeline ffitch, Paul Lisicky, and Zak Salih.

Writing a novel is a strange, emotionally unstable, wild undertaking! Many people held me up, listened, or otherwise made an impact on my writing life over the years it took to complete this book. Thank you, Jessica Adams, Erin Baillargeon, Jeff Bond, Heather Chriscaden, Lisa Dillon, Joe DiResta, Linda Hanlon, the Irish family, Samantha Isasi, the "Kittens," Patrick Ryan, Elana Stein (and everyone in the UHS Program at the University at Albany), Jared and Leigh Widjeskog, and Kyle Winkler. Thank you to my incredible extended family.

Thank you, Ellis Rowlands, who let me talk too much, and cry, and work out problems on our walks.

Suzanne Staub and Morgan Irish, you are my sisters.

Thank you, Lisa Koosis, for coaching me during the writing of the first draft of this book.

Thank you to the Juniper Summer Writing Institute at the University of Massachusetts Amherst and to everyone I learned from there.

I would not be a writer without the influence of my mother, a lifelong reader. This book is both our dreams. Thank you to my father and my brother for knowing I could do this, even when it seemed like I wasn't doing it.

Thank you, George Whitmore (1945–1989).

Finally: Thank you, Mark, for letting me be the isolated weirdo in the attic for five years as I wrote this novel, and for believing in me all the time. I love you.

RICHARD MIRABELLA is a writer and civil servant living in Upstate New York. His short stories have appeared in *Story*, *American Short Fiction* online, *One Story*, *Split Lip Magazine*, and elsewhere. *Brother & Sister Enter the Forest* is his first novel.